THE MESSAGE OF
KABĪRA'S BĪJAKA

R. K. JHA   MANJU

BLUEROSE PUBLISHERS
India | U.K.

Copyright © R. K. Jha and Manju 2024

All rights reserved by author. No part of this publication may be reproduced, stored in a retrieval system or transmitted in any form or by any means, electronic, mechanical, photocopying, recording or otherwise, without the prior permission of the author. Although every precaution has been taken to verify the accuracy of the information contained herein, the publisher assumes no responsibility for any errors or omissions. No liability is assumed for damages that may result from the use of information contained within.

BlueRose Publishers takes no responsibility for any damages, losses, or liabilities that may arise from the use or misuse of the information, products, or services provided in this publication.

For permissions requests or inquiries regarding this publication, please contact:

BLUEROSE PUBLISHERS
www.BlueRoseONE.com
info@bluerosepublishers.com
+91 8882 898 898
+4407342408967

ISBN: 978-93-5741-527-9

Cover Design: Tahira
Typesetting: Pooja Sharma

First Edition: March 2024

Dedication

Most humbly and devotedly, we dedicate this volume to the Omnipresent yet Transcendent Almighty and his benevolent illustrious personification, Kabīra, who mercifully showed the world the path to immortal bliss and freedom.

Acknowledgement

This work is an embodiment of the blessings of so many respected academicians who played a critical role in giving shape to its focus and contours. But, before showing our gratitude to all of them, we would like to heartily thank Indian Council of Philosophical Research, New Delhi, for sponsoring the research project on Kabīra's Bījaka, on which this volume is largely based. We lovingly recall the blessings of late Prof. N.S.S. Raman in encouraging us to go ahead with this research project and we express our deepest gratitude to him. We would also like to express our sincere gratitude to Prof. R.C. Pradhan, without whose beneficent cooperation our study of Kabīra's Bījaka could not have materialized. We also take this opportunity to record our gratitude to Prof. Bhuvan Chandel, Prof. Jodh Singh and Prof. H.S. Prasad for helping us in various ways in the formulation and materialization of this study. Last but not the least, we would also like to thank our daughters, Nitya and Sadhyaa, for helping us in all possible ways during the finalization of the manuscript.

Preface

The advent of Kabīra has left a tremendous impact on all sections of the Indian society. His teachings gave the proper direction and rejuvenation to the social and religious life of the Indian population. All sections of society accept him as a saint of the highest order. However, his preaching has been generally treated as just a religious and spiritual sermon. The philosophical content and depth of his thoughts have not been properly highlighted as yet. Even a casual study of his teachings readily shows the potential of studying the elements of metaphysics, epistemology, ethics, spiritualism, etc. in his thoughts. Therefore, a serious philosophical study of his teachings, as given in his Bījaka, has been taken up in this volume. His Bījaka has been selected as the basis of this study since it is universally accepted as the most authentic collection of his teachings.

The present study promises to be very relevant and significant because the life and teachings of Kabīra were explicitly devoted to the realization of social cohesion, based on love and understanding. One cannot overstate the urgent need for such love and understanding in the present society and the world at large. Kabīra had strived not just for the cohesion of the Hindu society but rather for the cohesion of the *ārya* and *anārya* sections of the society. Further, the life and teachings of Kabīra illustrate the true spirit of religion and spirituality, bereft of its outer garb of rituals and punditry. He emphasized again and again the universal possibility of the intuitive realization of the highest spiritual truth. Thus, he showed the true spiritual and religious goal, along with its means. Such true spirituality is the fountain-head of love, understanding, service, humility and wisdom and as such, it is the need of all ages. He had also emphasized the necessity of practising the basic ethical values such as truthfulness, non-violence, etc. for both worldly and spiritual purposes. He could not tolerate the practice of rites and rituals pitted against the basic ethical values, even in the name of religion and tradition. He also pointed out the importance of attaining true knowledge and realization for the spiritual well-being of all persons as well as for the harmony of society. Most importantly, he had emphasized that true knowledge and realization are a matter of innermost conviction that inevitably manifests itself at the levels of thought, speech, and action. Knowledge is never a matter of dry theoretical understanding alone. True knowledge absorbs our whole being and gets reflected in our actions. As such, a serious philosophical study of Kabīra's teachings is long overdue, wherein the stature and uniqueness of his thought may be brought out in a clear manner.

Contents

Chapter I: Kabīra: The Multi-faceted Saint 1

Chapter II: The Ultimate Reality 20

Chapter III: Spiritual Ignorance and Existential Bondage 49

Chapter IV: Spiritual Enlightenment and Liberation 79

Chapter V: The Towering Uniqueness of Kabīra 111

Chapter I

Kabīra: The Multi-faceted Saint

Kabīra truly illustrated the very literal meaning of the term 'Kabīra.' The word 'Kabīra' has an Arabic origin, which means 'great,' involving implicitly the connotation of divinity. The sacred *Koran* had shown this very word at first sight to the Muslim priest who had done the naming ceremony of baby Kabīra.[1] In retrospect, it can be easily seen that perhaps no other name could have done greater justice to the historical personality of Kabīra.

Kabīra epitomized the most exalted elements of both the Hindu and Islamic religious traditions, bereft of the outer garb of their rituals and orthodoxy. That itself was a commendable feat since the period of Kabīra was dominated by both Hindu orthodoxy and Islamic fanaticism. True philosophical and spiritual quests had been relegated to near oblivion. The ruling priestly classes were suppressing and exploiting the vast majority socially, economically and spiritually. As such, the suppressed majority was eagerly awaiting any light of love and knowledge that could give them some hope and dignity. At this point of time Kabīra rose up to the historical need and fulfilled his spiritual destiny. He had a good following among both the Hindus and the Muslims but his detractors definitely outnumbered his followers. It is not surprising to find therefore that in his long life Kabīra had to face many instances of social ostracism and political persecution as well. Despite all these challenges Kabīra staunchly stuck to his convictions and set an example for his followers.

Our information about Kabīra's life comes primarily from the scattered accounts given by his followers and admirers in their various works. There are numerous differences in their accounts, yet some important facts emerge rather coherently. Kabīra was born on the full-moon day of *jyeṣṭha* month in *samvat* 1455, i.e. 1398 AD.[2] Most of the accounts tell us that he was born in a Muslim weaver family but a minority section differs and holds that he was actually born in a Hindu family but abandoned due to fear of social ostracism and then he was later on discovered and adopted by a weaver couple, Nīrū and Nīmā, near the forests of Varanasi. Some go to the extent of saying that a divine light transformed into the form of baby Kabīra in the present day *Lahara-tārā* lake of Varanasi and there itself he was discovered by the weaver couple. However, the fact remains that Kabīra was brought up in a Muslim family of weavers in Varanasi.[3] His father's name was Nīrū and mother's name was Nīmā. Kabīra had not received any formal education. He had spent his childhood playfully and grew up to become a weaver. In time he was married to Loī and had a son and a daughter, named Kamāla and Kamālī. There are some accounts which suggest that Kabīra was rather disenchanted with his children. Despite his economic hardships Kabīra always struggled to meet his worldly obligations towards his family through the honest means of weaving clothes. In the midst of all these stressful conditions Kabīra also managed to be charitable towards the needy people. He became a disciple of Swāmī Rāmānanda and received from him the sacred *mantra* of *Rāma-nāma*.[4] In the guidance of Rāmānanda, Kabīra's simple and sincere mind gained deep spiritual insights into the nature of the Self, the supreme Reality, as well as that of the ordinary phenomenal world. Firmly believing in the truth of his own spiritual insights Kabīra set out to fulfill a great and difficult task, namely that of the social and spiritual rejuvenation of the masses. He gathered his following but also drew the ire of vested social, political, economic and religious groups. There are descriptions of the atrocities committed on Kabīra by the then Delhi Sultan, Sikandar Lodhi, during his visit to Varanasi where Kabīra was pitted against a mad elephant and he was also chained and thrown into the Ganges.[5] However, he miraculously emerged unscathed from these ordeals to prove his spiritual stature and humble the egotistic Sultan.

Kabīra had traveled extensively in his long life of 120 years.[6] He spread the message of social equality and spiritual realization to one and all, without any distinction of caste, creed and gender. His death was as dramatic as his birth and life. There is a popular belief among the Hindus that those who die within the sacred boundaries of Varanasi get liberation just on account of that, whereas people dying at Maghar are damned to hell. Maghar is a place across the Ganges, around six miles outside the sacred bounds of Varanasi. Kabīra traveled six miles to reach Magahar from Varanasi and there he gave up his physical body to attain *samādhi*. He had earlier pointed out that self-realization alone can give liberation, irrespective of whether one dies in Varanasi or Magahar.[7] He lived out his conviction. There are also accounts that after his *samādhi* there was a tussle between his Hindu and Muslim disciples over the point whether his dead body should be cremated or buried. However, when they removed the cloth covering his body there were only flowers to be found.[8] That put an end to their tussle and they divided the flowers among themselves. Thus, even after his physical death Kabīra preached tolerance, peace and the futility of fighting over mere rituals.

Before discussing the specific aspects of Kabīra's personality as a philosopher, saint and reformer, it is perhaps necessary to discuss briefly the inter-relationship of philosophy, spiritualism and reformist activities. It will provide us a better appreciation of Kabīra's holistic personality and endeavours.

The term philosophy comes from the Greek word *'philosophia'* which broadly means 'love of wisdom'. The basic connotation of the word 'philosophy' involves an explicit emphasis on the use of rational methods to understand our world, as also ourselves. The earlier western philosophical tradition had a definite stress upon understanding the world as compared to understanding ourselves. Moreover, it was considered necessary to have that understanding in a rational and linguistic framework.

In the context of the Indian tradition the term used is *'darśana'*. The connotation of *'darśana'* is not exactly the same as that of 'philosophy'. There are some points of agreement but also many points of divergence between them. *'Darśana'* literally means 'to see' or 'the sight' (of something). It is imperative to appreciate the vast difference between seeing something and explaining it rationally in so many words. A person may distinctly see the beauty of a flower or feel the sweetness of a mango but the same person may be totally at a loss to explain rationally that objective beauty and sweetness as well as their subjective experience. Thus, it is clear that we have the natural capacity of 'seeing' or experiencing various facts of the world even though it may be very difficult or even impossible for us to explicate rationally the nature, process and justification of those experiences. We can enjoy the taste of a mango and also derive nourishment from it even without rationally understanding that entire process. To seek a rational explanation of everything betrays our uncritical presupposition that each and every fact and experience of the universe must have its own rational justification. We enmesh ourselves in the web of our own imagined universal rationality.

The Indian tradition of *darśana* was rightly aware of this pitfall and thus it focused upon the need and methods of experiencing, *'seeing'* and benefiting from the vision of Reality. However, *darśana* involves both the subject and the object of the vision. This means there is a necessary place for duality in *darśana* due to which there always remains the possibility of inter-subjective rational argumentation and differences in the framework of language. However, in contrast with the western traditional philosophy, the avowed purpose of the entire exercise of *darśana* is not to arrive at some final rational explanation, even though it may remain as a contingent possibility. The focus of the Indian tradition is to directly *see* and experience Reality and thus benefit from it. It is immaterial whether that experience is amenable to rational and linguistic explanations or not. The tradition of *darśana* also emphasizes the personal and intuitive nature of that experience. Nothing can competently replicate that experience at the plane of language and rationality.

Thus, the discipline of *darśana* usually proceeds from the rational and linguistic plane since that is where the common man reposes his naive faith. It is utterly preposterous to think of transcending it in the beginning itself. However, it is to be used like a ladder and ultimately discarded after reaching the top. The avowed aim of *darśana* is the spiritual enlightenment of the individual by means of direct intuitive realization. Yet, the dualistic format of *darśana* leaves room for descriptions, arguments and elaborations. They are explicitly needed while interacting with other people, irrespective of their spiritual status. The use of language and rationality during inter-subjective discourses can hardly be wished away. This gives rise to the formal structure of different traditions of *darśana,* which are all meant for guiding the spiritual aspirant. However, the realization in which that spiritual quest culminates, totally transcends language and rationality but again while giving guidance to others, the necessity of resorting to language and rationality crops up. Thus, the goal and method of the Indian tradition of *darśana* is definitely not identical with that of philosophy. Yet, we are making use of the term 'philosophy' for *'darśana'* due to its popular contemporary usage. However, while doing so we should not overlook the above-mentioned differences between them.

The term used for spiritualism in the Indian tradition is *'adhyātma',* which is made up of two words *'adhi'* and *'ātma'*. The term *'ātma'* means the self, whereas *'adhi'* is a prefix with the connotation that something is grounded in or based upon something. As such, the term *'adhyātma'* has the basic meaning of 'being grounded in the self'. This term has a very wide range of application since there can be a possible spiritual *(ādhyātmika)* perspective of each and every aspect of our life for the simple reason that all of them necessarily require the involvement of our self. The focus of spiritualism or *adhyātma* is the self. It seeks to realize the true nature of the self as also its place in the universe. The effort to attain such self-realization is through the continuous process of self-reformation at the levels of thought, speech and action. One may get hints about the directions of self-reformation from a spiritual master having self-realization. During the preliminary stages of spiritual quest, intellectual argumentations at the rational and linguistic plane usually have a role to play. In this task the formal structure of the various traditions of *darśana* lend a helping hand. People usually need to be satisfied rationally and intellectually due to their uncritical naive belief in the necessity of rational consistency and justifications. However, it is not impossible for a person of immense spiritual strength to completely overthrow such naive belief in one go and have faith in the words of the realized master. The path of intellectual argumentations and whimsical spiritual experimentations is fraught with endless possibilities and thus uncertainty. Therefore, the Indian spiritual tradition strongly recommends accepting the guidance of some realized master or *Guru,* who may or may not be physically alive, for what is important is having faith in his words and accepting his guidance in one's spiritual quest for self-realization. A spiritual journey without the help of a realized master is like traversing an uncharted territory where one does not even know where he wants to go, much less through which path. All spiritual masters declare unanimously that the path of honest self-reformation alone can lead to the goal of self-realization. To accept the spiritual guidance of such masters one must have faith in the *Guru*, even though it may be of a hypothetical or implicit nature. Thus, in the pre-realization state one's self-reformation is faith based and somewhat deliberate in nature. It requires restraint *(nigraha),* austerity *(tapasyā),* discrimination *(viveka)* and faith *(śraddhā).* Such prolonged self-reformation finally culminates in the highest experience of a personal and intuitive self-realization, giving that person an indubitable proof of the nature of the Self and its place in the universe vis-à-vis other subjects and objects. Such intuitive experience transcends logic, language and rationality and it remains the most indubitable experience possible. A fundamental transformation in the personality of the spiritual aspirant takes place in that moment of self-realization. Such realization occurs in a moment despite the fact that it usually requires a prolonged period of self-reformation. Either a person has that highest intuitive realization or he does not have it. There is no third possibility with reference to that culminative intuitive experience. In the post-realization spiritual stage, all the aberrations and complexities of one's personality are completely erased and thus there remains no need for any more effort towards self-reformation. That is, in the moment of such supreme realization, a complete and irreversible reformation takes place, as a result of which the realized person exhibits all the spiritual perfections and virtues in a natural and instinctive manner. He effortlessly becomes the embodiment of all spiritual values.

After completing one's self-reformation in a perfect manner and achieving thereby the highest intuitive realization of the

Self, when the realized spiritual master brings down his individual consciousness to the level of the phenomenal world, he faces an entirely new task. That is the task of showing the path of spiritual enlightenment to the people wobbling in ignorance of the true Self.

Usually, the highest intuitive realization does not immediately bring about the cessation of physical body and existence. Even the realized masters continue to live at the physical plane, retaining the epistemic semblance of their individual consciousness, until the full exhaustion of their *prārabdha karma*. *Prārabdha karma* refers to those *karma* which are responsible for the various experiences of the present physical life, which means they have already started giving their results. *Prārabdha karma* may thus be called the 'already fructifying karma.' The stage in which the spiritual master has already won the highest realization but his physical existence continues due to the force of *prārabdha karma* is a state of 'liberation-while-alive' or *jīvanmukti*. In this stage the realized master does cognize the world of space-time and plurality, as also his own individuality *(ahaṃkāra),* but he is not misled by all this even for an instant. He has seen the Self and its Reality most proximately and therefore, even later on, he always looks through the cosmic illusion of the phenomenal world. A person acquainted with the appearance and mechanism of a mirage never runs after it in the hope of water despite the fact that he is definitely witnessing that mirage. An illusion exposed no longer remains so; it just becomes a strange phenomenon.

Himself being rid of the cosmic illusion, the spiritual master sets out to make others see that illusion and thus have that highest self-realization. However, he faces a strange problem. Self-realization requires perfect self-reformation but it is extremely difficult to convince and motivate people to reform themselves drastically by giving up their worldly ways and crooked thinking. They have their minds fixed on amassing phenomenal pleasures for themselves and their yardstick for truth is hinged on to logic, language, rationality and sensory experiences. On the other hand, self-realization requires giving up all worldly attachments. Moreover, the nature of Self i.e., the highest Reality, transcends the parameters of logic, language and rationality. Under these conflicting circumstances the spiritual master faces the challenge of guiding the spiritually ignorant people. He takes recourse to a number of techniques to achieve this end. He may point out the necessarily inconclusive nature of all worldly pursuits. He may even show how such pursuits ultimately boomerang, giving pain and frustration instead of the desired peace and happiness. He may also point out the passing nature of phenomenal existence. He may also try to prove, by cajoling people into the experimental practice of meditation, how their mind is a slave of various external stimuli. He may then prod them to overcome their slavery of matter and become truly independent. He may try to motivate them for achieving self-realization even by pointing out that the core elements desired under the cloak of all worldly pursuits, namely existence, consciousness, bliss and power, are to be found in an infinite and permanent manner within the Self alone. Most importantly, the spiritual master presents himself as a living embodiment of peace, poise, contentment, bliss, knowledge, power, love, mercy, etc. in order to prove the positive benefits of self-realization, irrespective of the surrounding material circumstances. To this end, he may also sometimes exhibit his transcendence of the usual phenomenal laws of space, time and causality in the form of some so-called miracles. The purpose however remains only to motivate the spiritually ignorant masses to reform themselves so that they may have self-realization and thus enjoy the eternal bliss and majesty of the Self.

While trying to motivate the masses in these various possible ways, the spiritual master is forced to make use of logic, language and rationality as that is the initial operational plane of the masses. He points out the puzzling and conflicting nature of worldly life, sometimes pointedly and sometimes through parables and allegories. While trying to discuss the nature of the true Self or the highest Reality the spiritual master is often forced to make such use of language that appears to go against ordinary logic and rationality. However, that is the best bet on two counts. Firstly, being imperative to indicate somehow the nature of the highest Reality to satisfy the preliminary curiosity of the spiritual aspirants, it is perhaps better to give even an imperfect indication rather than not giving any at all. The latter eventuality would lead to utter chaos and easily sabotage the entire spiritual program. Secondly, such supra-logical use of language brings out the limitations of ordinary logic and language in dealing with the nature of the highest Reality. This may then serve to shake or even uproot the naive faith of those people in the validity of ordinary logic and language. Moreover, it may also convey to them, even though theoretically, the transcendent nature of the highest Reality.

Putting together all the pointed and oblique talks of the spiritual master gives rise to the contours of a philosophical framework, which is most likely not to have a rigorous logical consistency. However, that is not a drawback as it only shows that it is not intended to be a logical framework dealing with some ordinary phenomenon in the first place. Its loose logical structure is necessary to reflect the supra-logical transcendent nature of the highest Reality or the Self.

The realized spiritual master sees all the beings in the world with an even eye. He is equally moved by the suffering of the beggar and the king and also, he is equally unforgiving of their foolishness and egoism. He applies the same yardstick to judge both the downtrodden castes and the priestly castes. He unhesitatingly criticizes whatever he finds to be out of tune with the nature of the highest Reality and its manner of manifestation in the phenomenal world. This often pits him against the influential and exploitative groups and institutions of his times. All this unwittingly but inevitably makes him a crusader of social, economic, political and religious reforms.

Thus, it is clear that there is a deep inter-relationship between the Indian tradition of philosophy *(darśana)*, spiritualism *(adhyātma)* and various kinds of reforms. Philosophy, spiritualism and reforms are three stages of the same process, where each one logically culminates in the next one. The personality of Kabīra was truly holistic in this sense as he traversed the entire logical series to exhibit the inter-related facets of a philosopher, saint and reformer. His utterances shake our intellect and give us food for thought. He also tells us how to reform ourselves for the purpose of attaining the highest realization. Last but not the least, he also tells us how to live in society and behave with our fellow beings. He tells us about the true values of a spiritually enlightened society. In doing all this, Kabīra gave back to society the maximum possible benefits of his self-realization.

Kabīra: The Philosopher

Just like a true philosopher Kabīra was eager to attain the highest possible knowledge. However, he was not to be satisfied with any piece of ordinary intellectual knowledge. He had heard about the possibility of a higher kind of intuitive knowledge that gives an immediate insight into the fundamental nature of each and every thing in the universe. That possibility obviously attracted the philosophical mind of Kabīra and he set out on the path of spiritual realization. He achieved it in due course of time and also declared publicly the truth of its universal validity. He considered all other knowledge to be inferior as compared to that supreme realizational knowledge.[9]

Kabīra was not a blind superstitious person who could go on accepting anything and everything endlessly just on the basis of faith. He had the highest regard for his spiritual preceptor, Swāmī Rāmānanda, but that could not oblige him to accept all that his *Guru* believed in. For him the highest and most necessary criterion of the acceptability of some idea was a corresponding personal experience,[10] whether at the ordinary material plane or at the higher intuitive one, as the case may be. He preached the same highest criterion of acceptability to all his followers as well.

On the basis of his own intuitive experience Kabīra had declared that the true nature of our own inner consciousness or light is quite identical with the highest cosmic Reality.[11]

He described the individual consciousness as the microcosmic manifestation *(piṇḍa)* of the macrocosmic Reality *(brahmāṇḍa)*.[12] That is, he believed that all the transcendent qualities of Brahman are also latent in the individual consciousness but they are covered by the veil of ignorance. To realize those qualities, that ignorance has to be removed through the practice of spiritual disciplines.

Kabīra highlighted the need of philosophical reflections as the first step towards spiritual progress. He always pointed out the inevitable pattern of all worldly pursuits, where the cycle of prolonged efforts, uncertain achievements and definite disillusionment is repeated over and over again. A reflective study of the worldly life can save us from falling into this trap.

Kabīra accepted the need of having a *Guru* for making progress in the right direction but at the same time he also pointed out the absolute requirement for the *Guru* to have proper spiritual realization.[13] One blind person cannot lead another blind person to the desired destination. Faith in the *Guru* cannot be a substitute for true realization on the part of the *Guru*. Kabīra knew very well that misplaced faith amounts to mere superstition and that is all the more degrading and precarious.

Kabīra pointed out the superiority of a living *Guru* for the purpose of spiritual guidance but he was also willing to accept the words of earlier realized masters. That is why he accepted the authority of the Vedas. But more than the authority of the Vedas or any living *Guru* he valued the authenticity of one's own intuitive experiences.

Kabīra had a clear intuitive experience of the absolute and immutable nature of the highest Reality. With respect to that

Reality, everything in the phenomenal world is just its epistemic and illusory manifestation.[14] However, Kabīra is also clear on the point that the ontological stuff and consciousness involved in these epistemic illusions is nothing but the absolute Brahman itself.[15]

Kabīra has also given a clear criterion to understand the defining characteristic of the highest Reality. He says that anything which has a point of beginning and goes through real changes is but a passing phenomenon, a product of *māyā*.[16] Only that which is never born and is ontologically immutable should be considered truly Real. A detailed study of the philosophical elements contained in Kabīra's utterances will be taken up in the succeeding chapters.

Kabīra: The Saint

Kabīra was a living example of the complete transformation of one's personality following the attainment of the supreme self-realization. The thorough transformation brought about by such realization gets reflected at the levels of thought, speech and action. The saintly qualities of Kabīra's personality were the natural and necessary consequences of his supreme spiritual realization.

Kabīra, the saint, was the embodiment of universal and unconditional love and mercy. He did not make any distinction on the basis of caste, creed, gender or economic status. For him, each and every being was but an individual manifestation of the same Brahman.[17] As such, his universal love and mercy was actually his manner of interaction with the extended universal Self. He staunchly believed that no true saint could ever make a distinction between his own self and that of other beings. Such an even behaviour is the hallmark of true spiritual realization.

As a saint Kabīra also professed and practised various spiritual values such as austerity, forgiveness, contentment, fearlessness, dispassion, discrimination, etc. He also emphasized the necessity of practising these as spiritual disciplines for the sake of spiritual realization. He repeatedly pointed out the futility of running after sensory enjoyments and thus advised people to develop control of mind.

Modesty was the most important saintly characteristic of Kabīra. He was not ashamed to declare himself as being comparable to the particles of dust lying at the feet of realized masters. He had also described himself as the obedient dog of God, doing everything at his behest alone.[18] By doing all this Kabīra wished to convey the necessity of giving up pride and egotism of all sorts. Egotism and spiritual realization never go hand in hand.

Kabīra highlighted the spiritual values of simplicity and honesty not only through words but also through practice. He was convinced that a crooked and cunning person can never make any spiritual advancement. Thus, he highlighted the necessity of practising truthfulness.

He also pointed out the spiritual importance of continence since a mind engrossed in the grossest form of sensory enjoyment cannot make any spiritual progress.[19] Moreover, he also pointed out the importance of overcoming the limitless desire for wealth since material wealth is the means of obtaining various sensory pleasures in the world. Thus, the lust for wealth actually signifies the lust for various sensory pleasures. Moreover, it is essential to overcome this lust for wealth because being endless in nature its pursuit devours all our time and energy, leaving us with no possibility of spiritual engagement.

Kabīra also pointed out that the path of spiritual realization is fraught with the severest of challenges. Only the bravest can hope for success in this field. He says one must be prepared to sacrifice all for the sake of spiritual realization. The goal of spiritual realization demands our highest priority. There cannot be any compromise on this count.

Kabīra also exhibited his devotional attitude towards God. He considered God as that manifestation of the supreme Brahman which is responsible for all the affairs of the phenomenal world, beginning with its (epistemic) creation and going up to its final dissolution.[20] He pleaded to God for divine mercy with the varied attitudes of a son, a friend, a servant, a beloved, etc. He was quite emphatic about the absolute necessity of winning the grace of God and one's *Guru* for achieving the highest spiritual realization.

Kabīra's self-realization was the fountain-head of his saintly nature and his saintly personality got reflected in his philosophical outlook as well as in his varied reformist comments and activities.

Kabīra: The Reformer

The reformist utterances and activities of Kabīra were the direct outcome of his exalted spiritual realization. He could not restrain himself from pointing out any fault whenever he came across something spiritually demeaning and objectionable, irrespective of the status of its perpetrator. Kabīra was a vocal critic of the orthodox caste system.[21] He pointed out that all human beings were both physiologically and spiritually alike. Therefore, there was no basis for the caste system. It was only a degrading socio-religious institution for facilitating the exploitation of the lower castes by the upper ones.

He also used to point out rather bluntly the foolishness of maintaining animosity towards other religious groups and sects.[22] He said there is only one God. It is just that it is called differently by different religious groups. Everybody prays to the same God ultimately and therefore there can be no greater folly than fighting among ourselves in the name of God.

Kabīra used to severely criticize the orthodoxy and ritualistic hypocrisy of both the Hindu and Muslim priestly classes.[23] He used to make fun of their activities and say that they knew nothing about God. He used to say that God is present within all beings and therefore the loving service of the needy and downtrodden people is the highest worship of God.

He was also very critical about the killing of animals for the sake of food and ritual sacrifices.[24] He said that killing animals and eating them was nothing short of demonic behaviour. Sacrificing them for the sake of religious rituals is equally inexcusable as God can never be pleased to see pain and violence inflicted of innocent animals. He said if it is believed that the sacrificed animals win the heavens then the priests should rather sacrifice their own near and dear ones. He was disgusted to see such meaningless violence and said that it is nothing but catering to one's demonic appetites by perversely using the name of God and religion.

Kabīra also used to mock at the foolishness of amassing too much wealth, as such people cannot make full use of their wealth for their own purposes. Also, they are often unwilling to use them for charitable purposes. Therefore, they just keep it lying idle and then ultimately, they are forced to leave it all behind at the time of death. As such, Kabīra used to say that one should try to be content with minimal material resources but one should never be a miser while giving financial help to the needy people.[25] Spending money for welfare purposes purifies the mind by diminishing our selfish engagements and it thus paves the path of spiritual progress.

Thus, the reformist aspect of Kabīra's personality was very comprehensive. He had addressed various social, economic, political and religious problems of his times and in turn he earned the enmity of the vested interests. In spite of that, he never stopped from saying the truth and criticizing the objectionable practices of his times.

In this way the personality of Kabīra was multi-faceted, exhibiting the traits of a philosopher, a saint and a reformer of the highest caliber. Yet, it must not be overlooked that the mainspring of all these varied activities was undoubtedly his supreme self-realization. Therefore, he was unequivocal in declaring that our first duty as human beings is the attainment of self-realization. It must be accorded our highest priority.

Chapter II

The Ultimate Reality

Kabīra was not a mere speculative intellectual philosopher but a self-realized saint of the highest order. His insight into the nature of the supreme reality was rooted in his own meditative and intuitive experiences. As a result, his conception of supreme reality is definitely a very esoteric and intuitive one. In the present project we are trying to understand Kabīra's outlook on the basis of his most important work, namely the Bījaka.

The reality has been described, rather indicated, in various ways in the Bījaka. To get a broad understanding of the different ways in which it has been indicated we will take some selective passages from the Bījaka and see what has been explicitly and implicitly described in them.

The very beginning of the Ramainī chapter of Bījaka[26] indicates the various aspects of the supreme reality. In the transcendent aspect it has been described as the light that exists internally within all of us. It is the subtle light of reality. Secondly, it is also described as the subtle vibration responsible for bringing about the manifestation of the world. Moreover, it is also described as the cosmic creative energy, depicted as a feminine principle *(nārī),* which is responsible for the epistemic projection of the entire universe. At the same time, this supreme reality which has both transcendent and projective aspects, is also described as the grounds over which the triple aspects or the three cosmic deities, Hari, Brahmā and Tripurāri or Śaṅkara, come about and they are responsible for the sustenance, creation and destruction of the worlds respectively. These three deities are so many manifestations of the same supreme reality, as projected with the help of the cosmic projective energy.

Immediately after this Kabīra points out[27] that the same cosmic creative energy, the cosmic *nārī,* is also responsible for projecting various masculine and feminine principles in the universe. These various masculine and feminine principles also represent the active and passive aspects, or the cognizing and cognized aspects, of the universe. In short, that cosmic principle is also responsible for epistemically projecting various subjective and objective principles of the world. The dualistic universe gets projected because of this principle alone. Kabīra also says that the real nature and extent of this cosmic energy is absolutely unfathomable. Nobody can know its true limits by any means.

The ninth line of the same stanza[28] brings out the irony of the situation that the entire world has been epistemically projected by the one creative principle and yet we are living in a world which is usually taken to be pluralistic in nature and we believe in the difference of one thing from the other things, as also of ourselves from the other beings. This is truly amazing because there is but one source of all this.

The eleventh line of the same stanza[29] brings out the inexpressible nature of the supreme reality, as also its manner of epistemic manifestation in the world. Kabīra says, that which is the ontological absolute, that which is beyond all changes, seems to be epistemically bringing about the entire world and this is truly amazing. On the one hand, it is an ontological absolute and on the other hand, it alone is responsible for the creative manifestation of the world. In this situation it is very difficult to exactly express in words and concepts the nature of that supreme reality. Kabīra says that even if one were granted a million tongues it would still be an impossible task to truly describe the nature of supreme reality and its manner of deliberation in the world.

The thirteenth line[30] brings out the illusory nature of the dualistic world, as compared to the ontologically supreme reality and Kabīra says that the entire world of duality is non-existent or illusory. It is only the supreme reality that is the truth. As long as one does not know this fact there is no way that one can escape from the miserable cycle of transmigration and suffering.

The first line of the next stanza[31] is very significant because it points out that the *jīva* is nothing but a microcosmic manifestation of the same transcendent and supreme reality. Moreover, that *jīva* alone is responsible for the manifestation of consciousness in our various cognitive activities. As such, our cognitive activities become possible by virtue of the pure consciousness characterizing that supreme reality.

The next line[32] points out that the cosmic projective principle, which is none other than the supreme reality itself, is actually responsible for epistemically projecting the world, arising out of its desire for such manifestation. This primordial energy manifests itself in the form of three cosmic energies - *sattva, rajas* and *tamas* - and therefore, it is also understandable as *Gāyatrī,* whose first three quarters represent the three cosmic qualities or energies and also the three realms of the dualistic universe.

The next line[33] goes on to say that in accordance with the nature of these three basic energies which represent the nature of that cosmic energy, there is the manifestation of the three deities who are directly responsible for the phenomenal creation, sustenance and destruction of the world. They are Brahmā, Viṣṇu and Maheśa, responsible for the creation, sustenance and destruction respectively of the phenomenal worlds. All these three deities are like the sons of that primordial energy. The next two lines of the same stanza[34] present a cosmic irony. It says, Brahmā asked that primordial energy, "Oh Mother, who is your husband?" and that primordial energy replied "There is no one else apart from you and me; in fact, you are my husband and I am your wife." This passage actually brings out the fact that the energy which is responsible for the epistemic projection of these deities is also actively associated with the functioning of these deities. They are able to perform their tasks only due to the energy coming to them from that primordial energy. Moreover, that primordial energy is not ontologically separate either from the supreme reality or from the epistemic manifestations of that reality in the form of the three cosmic deities. As such, that cosmic projective energy is both the mother and the wife of these three principal deities.

The next line[35] brings out even more dramatically the various aspects of that cosmic energy. It says that She is the spouse of both the father and the son, where the term 'father' is referring to the supreme reality and the term 'son' is referring to the various manifestations of that reality, such as the three cosmic deities and the various *jīvas,* that are the microcosmic manifestations of that supreme reality. Now, that energy is the creative energy of the absolute reality, as well as the cognitive energy characterizing all of its manifestations, including the *jīvas*. In this sense, She is the inalienable energy or *śakti* of both the transcendent reality and the *jīvas* and this is a great cosmic wonder. Kabīra goes on to say that there are very few people who understand the nature of this primordial energy and truly recognize their own father, namely the supreme reality.

The very first line of the next stanza[36] wonders as to who was the one that existed first of all. In answer to this question Kabīra replies logically, "who else, but the one responsible for bringing about all that which succeeds it". He goes on to say that Brahmā, Viṣṇu and Maheśa, as also *Śakti,* appeared only later on. As such, the cause of all these alone can be taken as the first existent and the primordial cause. However, the manifested *jīvas* develop devotion towards these manifested deities naturally because that supreme reality is not tangible in a manner that these deities responsible for various functions of the world, namely creation, sustenance and destruction, are.

The next line of the same stanza[37] goes on to describe how that same *Māyā,* after the manifestation of the prime deities and the *jīvas,* brings about the epistemic projection of the various elements of the universe such as ether, air, fire, etc.

After that, the projection of the various spheres of the phenomenal universe took place.

The fifth stanza discusses the ways and means of getting out of this cosmic illusion, where even Brahmā fails to understand the nature of the supreme reality.[38] Kabīra says that two words have been given by tradition as the means of getting out of the cosmic illusion.[39] They are *anahada sabda (anāhata śabda)* and *joti (jyoti)*. *Anahada sabda* refers to the absolute vibration, indicating the transcendent reality, whereas *joti* refers to the transcendent light, the transcendent consciousness, once again indicating the supreme reality. The meditative practice regarding this supreme vibration and the inner light manifesting within all of us is the way out of this illusion. This tradition of meditation was upheld by the saints of earlier times and it had appealed to great ones like Sanaka and Sanandana. They represent the Vedic tradition of meditation for developing an insight into that supreme reality. This tradition clearly presents that higher reality as the absolute vibration and transcendent light. However, later on, the Vedic as well as the non-Vedic traditions elaborately developed this spiritual tradition in various directions and resulted in numerous devotional paths of realization.[40] These devotional traditions distinguished themselves from the other ones and as such, they developed their particular identities. They presented their own unique conceptions of the higher reality. However, due to their restricted vision and practices they could not accommodate the universal nature of that reality, which in turn led to a partial and distorted conception of that supreme reality.

The fifth line[41] points out the rare Vedic statements which say that the higher reality is to be introspected within our hearts and there lies the union of the *jīva* and the supreme reality. However, Kabīra says, there are but few who understand the true import of these statements and people subscribing to devotional paths having a dualistic outlook, have instead gone into the phenomenal interpretations of these statements. Accordingly, they have ascribed various phenomenal characterizations to the supreme reality and all this has ultimately led to their continued bondage in the transmigration cycle. Only the real preceptors have the capacity of getting the knowledge of non-duality and without such knowledge it is not possible to get rid of our dualistic convictions about the world. Through all ages, there have been different saints telling us about the non-dual and transcendent nature of the supreme reality. However, the unfortunate ones do not listen to them.

The sixth stanza[42] explains the reason for the inexpressibility of supreme reality. Kabīra wonders in what terms, that supreme reality, the cause of all else, should be described. There are no concepts or words which may be suitable for its description. Moreover, there was no one witnessing that supreme reality at the time when nothing else was projected out of it. If there was no cognizer of that reality in its primordial state, there can be no logical possibility of its description either. Even the *Oṁkāra,* considered as the root of all the Vedas, did not exist alongside that reality. That supreme reality existed as one alone. Therefore, there is no possibility of describing its nature and divisions.

The fourth line,[43] however, points out the way for a direct realization of that supreme reality, that transcendent light. Kabīra says that when the mind is in a natural state of absolute tranquility i.e. the state of the highest *samādhi,* then there is a spontaneous manifestation of that supreme reality in the form of inner light within ourselves. It is just the same as the transcendent and non-dual absolute reality. Kabīra says that reality is the self-caused cause of all else. He says one should realize this reality intuitively and understand the non-dual nature of the apparent dualistic world.

The seventh stanza[44] points out how difficult it is to describe the deliberations of that which is beyond all change and activity. There is no space or region to identify it. Moreover, whenever it is intuitively cognized, there are no characteristics qualifying it. As such, it is absolutely impossible to describe that reality; there are no terms for describing it.

The first line of the eighth stanza[45] refers to the *mahāvākya "tattvamasi"* which comes up in the Chāndogya upaniṣad and points out the absolute identity of the *jīva* and the supreme reality, Brahman. Kabīra says this is one of greatest conclusions of the Vedic tradition and it describes accurately the nature of relationship of the individual *jīvas* and the supreme reality. However, this great conclusion cannot be conveyed accurately by anyone who is unqualified to have such intuitive knowledge. Also, it should always be given only to those who are deserving of such esoteric knowledge. Eligibility for description and reception of this knowledge has great importance, since otherwise there can be no possibility of its proper comprehension.

In the twenty-first stanza[46] Kabīra brings out the nature of relationship between the absolute reality and its phenomenal manifestation in the form of *jīvas,* the phenomenal egos, which are involved in all kinds of dualistic activities. Kabīra points out that it is the absolute reality itself which is ultimately responsible for the epistemic creation, sustenance and destruction of everything in the world. It is that alone which is immanent in the various cosmic elements such as earth, water, etc. That reality is the truly attributeless supreme ontological reality.

In the twenty-sixth stanza[47] Kabīra compares the world and the supreme reality with a painting and the painter responsible for it. The painter alone is the real entity; the painting is just an external projection of his internal state. It does not have any existence apart from that reality. Fortunate are the souls who do not get misled by the pluralistic beauty of this world, the painting of the supreme reality, and instead, they are able to cognize intuitively the omnipresence and absoluteness of that supreme reality. They alone are successful in overcoming this phenomenal illusion.

The thirtieth stanza[48] significantly brings out an important distinction between the four Vedas and the different philosophical systems, namely the six orthodox systems, which derive their origin from the Vedic literature and yet they have gone astray. Kabīra says that all the six systems indulge in lots of rhetoric and make-believe. In doing so, they have lost their hold on the basic nature of reality. In fact, they have overlooked the point that the basic reality is not a matter of intellectual discussion or description. In this context, the Vedas seem to be more honest to the nature of that indescribable reality. Instead of directly describing that supreme reality, they rather describe the various phenomenal manifestations of that reality, along with the various deities responsible for the proper functioning of those manifestations. Thus, the silence of the Vedas regarding that absolute reality is more eloquent about its nature as compared to the elaborate discussions given by the six formal philosophical systems.

The thirty-seventh stanza[49] brings out the significance of the Bījaka. The term *'bījaka'* stands for an encoded direction about the place of some secret treasure. Kabīra says that the Bījaka is such an encoded description of the highest treasure, namely the supreme reality. However, it is an encoded information and therefore, if taken at its face value or in the literal sense, it is very difficult to understand the true implications of the Bījaka. One can grasp its real meaning only with the help of a realized preceptor.

The forty-first stanza[50] brings out the real distinction between a wise person and a fool. The criterion is, understanding the true nature of worldly suffering. Even though everyone claims to have his own particular understanding of the nature of suffering and the way out, it is only the person who understands that this suffering is on account of not realizing the internal presence of the supreme reality within us, who may be aptly called a wise person. He is the spiritually wise person who understands the immanence of that supreme and absolute reality.

The forty-second stanza[51] points out that in the pure state of the soul, which is non-distinct from the transcendent reality, everything was lying latent in it. There was no external manifestation even at the epistemic plane, not even the manifestation of *Īśvara* or the controlling deity of the phenomenal universe. In that situation Kabīra wonders how can a person having such higher realization get involved in any devotional practices towards that *Īśvara*. His realization would have taken him beyond the possibility of such devotional practices. Even when he may seem to be involved in some such practices, it is certain that at the inner plane he must be established only in the universal non-duality of that supreme reality.

Kabīra goes on to highlight the paramount importance of perfect truthfulness and honesty.[52] Kabīra says that those who are pure in heart and in whom there is perfect correspondence between the heart and the tongue, can easily get rid of the phenomenal illusion.

The sixty-third stanza[53] beautifully brings out the amazing picture of the cosmic illusion where the supreme reality becomes both the subjective and objective principles. It is also not different from the cosmic principle of epistemic projections, responsible for projecting the entire world. At the same time, that supreme reality is also immanent in each and every particle of the phenomenal universe. Kabīra says that the same reality, which makes everyone dance to the tune of cosmic illusion, itself also dances to the same tune in the form of the various *jīvas*. At the same time, it alone is present everywhere in all forms of manifestations occurring at the phenomenal plane. Thus, this line beautifully brings out the transcendence and immanence of the same supreme reality.

In the sixty-eighth stanza[54] of Ramainī, Kabīra brings out the great spiritual importance of the practice of meditation. It says that only those who are expert in the art of introspection, somewhat comparable to the difficult skill of an acrobat in the physical domain, have access to the intuitive realization of that supreme reality. It is only with closed eyes that one can behold that supreme reality manifesting within our souls. In the moment of that realization there is nothing else whatsoever apart from that great reality. This alone is the liberating non-dual knowledge and realization.

The seventy-seventh stanza[55] of Ramainī wonderfully brings out the inexpressible transcendent as well as immanent nature of the supreme reality. It says that the same supreme reality is also the grounds over which the entire universe is projected as its manifestation. The entire universe is nothing but an external epistemic projection of that reality itself. The basic nature of that reality as consciousness is the thing which is most adorable to everyone in the world. It is so because our own existence, the continuation of our cognitive status, is the dearest to us all. Further, it is not possible to identify that supreme reality and its phenomenal manifestation in the form of *jīvas* as either masculine or feminine. It is beyond the classification of gender. It is also beyond the possibilities of various descriptions because in the ontological sense, it is devoid of all characteristics and divisions. In spite of this, it alone is the reality which is universally immanent in everything. Also, it is not truly possible to understand its nature in terms of misery and bliss since it transcends both these relativistic concepts. At the same time, it is true that at the phenomenal plane the manifestation of that reality always seems involved with the experiences of bliss and suffering of various kinds. The nature and form of this reality, being inexpressible, is capable of being realized through various possible spiritual paths. However, among these numerous realizational paths, the pathway of knowledge is the most sublime one. Despite this, even the persons who have devoted themselves completely to the meditative realization of that reality, have come to the conclusion that it is not possible to gauge the true nature and extent of that supreme reality. Any amount of meditative insight is inherently incapable of fathoming that infinite supreme reality.

The first stanza[56] of the Śabda chapter brings out the wonderous situation that the same (feminine) creative principle, the cosmic *nārī*, gives birth to two masculine principles namely *Īśvara* and the numerous *jīvas*. This creative principle is also the energy characterizing the supreme reality. This mystery is to be understood by the people desirous of liberation, since without comprehending the nature of this projective principle, there is no possibility of getting out of the cosmic illusion.

In the fourth stanza[57] of the Śabda chapter Kabīra points out that the entire range of dualistic concepts, deliberating on the nature of reality and its phenomenal manifestations in terms of so many words, is just a chimera. It does not give the true understanding of that reality. In fact, that supreme reality is very simple and yet people often try to understand it in terms of complex expressions. The moment one gives up the complex approach to that reality and believes in the simplicity of heart and mind, effecting a perfect correspondence between the heart and the tongue, the mind achieves a natural state of tranquility. That tranquility, in turn, effects a spontaneous revelation of that supreme reality at the intuitive plane. However, such a simple way of approaching the supreme reality is often not acceptable to the people as they are accustomed to the complex ways of approaching things.

The fifth stanza[58] of the Śabda chapter describes the bewildering nature of the manifestation of that supreme reality. Kabīra says that if he were to speak the simple truth about that reality, hardly anyone would believe it. However, the fact of the matter is that the same cosmic principle, which is inalienably associated with that supreme reality, is also responsible for the epistemic projection of the world in terms of various sentient and insentient entities, as well as various subjective and objective principles. It is the reason behind the operation of various phenomenal and spiritual laws and it is because of this principle alone that the cycle of transmigration and suffering, as also the highest intuitive knowledge and liberation, become possible. Ultimately, the same supreme reality, by virtue of its cosmic creative principle, manifests itself in the form of various phenomenal entities that go through the phenomenal cycles and at the same time, that supreme reality also witnesses all these as the transcendent conscious principle. It is a truly bewildering scenario. It is not comprehensible to the phenomenal understanding. Only those who take refuge at the feet of the realized souls can hope of getting beyond this bewildering cosmic illusion.

The seventh stanza[59] of the Śabda chapter says it is extremely difficult to describe the nature of that supreme reality. If one were to describe it in terms of words and concepts of the phenomenal kind, it would be a gross misapplication. On the other hand, it is a fact that it is perfectly realizable at the intuitive plane. In this situation it emerges that the inexpressible is realizable, while the true nature of reality is not a matter of linguistic description and phenomenal understanding.

At the end of the eighth stanza[60] of the Śabda chapter Kabīra says that the ten divine incarnations, described in the various Purāṇas, truly belong to the phenomenal realm only. They belong to the realm of duality. They are subject to origination and destruction. As such, they cannot be uniquely identified with the transcendent reality, which is beyond all possibilities of mutability. That which is subject to change and decay can never be the absolute reality. It has to be necessarily a manifestation of the cosmic *māyā* alone. Even though that *māyā* is inseparable from the supreme reality, the same cannot be said about its projective manifestations. The ten incarnations may certainly be taken as representing certain divine qualities in an excellent manner at the phenomenal plane. Yet, they cannot be specifically identified with the supreme reality because they are its manifestations within the spatio-temporal world only.

The eighteenth stanza[61] of the Śabda chapter points out the unfathomable and inexpressible nature of the supreme reality, as also that of its characteristic projective and creative energy. Kabīra says that the spiritually ignorant folks can never hope to identify the true limits of that creative energy. Even the three principle cosmic deities, Brahmā, Viṣṇu and Maheśa, fail in this respect precisely because there are no limits of that creative principle. In this situation, one may well imagine the fate of the ordinary phenomenal beings. That is to say, it is a vain effort trying to ascertain the true nature and limits of the cosmic creative principle, as also that of the supreme reality, which it characterizes.

In the twenty-second stanza[62] of the Śabda chapter Kabīra pleads that we should give up our obsessive indulgence in various imagined concepts. True freedom can be obtained only by going beyond the realm of mere epistemic projections and imaginations. It requires the intuitive realization of the supreme ontological reality, the transcendent Brahman, which is utterly incomparable to all the phenomena. Without the realization of the immanence, the transcendence and the absolute nature of that supreme Brahman there can be no true liberation from the cosmic illusion.

In the twenty-seventh stanza[63] of the Śabda chapter Kabīra once again points out the amazing nature of the supreme reality as well as the fascinating state of its intuitive realization. Kabīra says that the supreme reality, despite its transcendence, is also immanent in each and every corner of the universe. The knowers of this supreme reality possess the highest bliss even though not possessing any worldly treasures. They may be very poor in the worldly sense, yet they do not suffer and grieve for their plight. They continuously enjoy the bliss of deep sleep, or rather a bliss even greater than that in the state in *samādhi* or the state of natural tranquility of the mind. Moreover, they witness the subtle light of that supreme reality everywhere in the world even though that light may not be localized at any one point of space, in the sense of the source of that universal illumination. Such people are the ones devoted to the attributeless form of the supreme reality. It is truly amazing to see that the entity most adored by the realized persons is such that it has no forms and attributes. This supreme reality is not at all accessible to the worldly-minded people.

Deprived of this supreme treasure, the worldly people are always suffering through the transmigratory cycle.

In the forty-third stanza[64] of the Śabda chapter Kabīra points out the futility of intellectual argumentations over the nature of that supreme reality. He says, "O wise ones, why are you deliberating upon the nature of that transcendent reality, where there is no creation and there is no creator? In that situation how can you understand its nature in the framework of dualistic concepts?" In the realm of that supreme reality there are no subtle or gross entities. There are no cosmic elements. There is no sun and there is no moon in that realm. There is no manifestation of even space and time. It is the pure transcendent light, the pure non-dual consciousness and it does not have any form. In this situation how can there be any linguistic description and phenomenal understanding of that reality? The nature of that supreme reality is not amenable to any religious practices. There can be no place for various rituals and sacred syllables in approaching it through intuitive realization. It is not even possible to decide whether it is a unity or a plurality. There are no divine beings, incarnations and preceptors in the realm of that supreme reality. The deliberations of even the Vedas do not describe it. It transcends the Vedas. The principal deities controlling the functions of the universe, as also the energies or *śaktis* associated with those deities, do not have any explicit manifestations in the realm of that supreme reality. There is no lineage with reference to which one may try to understand the existence and nature of that reality. The person realizing intuitively the nature of that transcendent reality becomes a true *jīvanmukta* and Kabīra says that it is always a matter of great pride and honour to be a disciple of such a person.

The seventy-fifth stanza[65] of the Śabda chapter points out the misleading nature of various phenomenal traditions, in the realms of both religious or ethical practices. The distinction of various religious traditions, the concept of righteousness of various actions and the distinctions based on gender, are all pertaining to the realm of phenomenal traditions and they do not refer at all to the nature of the supreme transcendent reality. The supreme reality is the universal ground for the manifestation of everything in the phenomenal realm. In that situation how can the various distinctions be truly representative of the common ground reality? The crux of the matter is that these distinctions pertain only to the phenomenal conventions and traditions. The nature of all phenomenal beings, in the physiological sense, is very much similar. Also, once the physical body is destroyed it is not possible to distinguish between the souls of persons belonging to the so-called different traditions. That is to say, the subtle conscious reality inhabiting the various physical beings is not distinguishable in terms of different religious traditions. The principal deities controlling the creation, sustenance and destruction of the phenomenal universe are representative of the three energies characterizing the cosmic creative principle. These energies alone are responsible for the phenomenal manifestations of various kinds and as such, there is a common fundamental nature of all the phenomenal entities. The distinctions of religion and other criteria is not reflective of the nature of the common ontological ground.

In the seventy-eighth stanza[66] of the Śabda chapter Kabīra says that the manner in which we understand the nature of reality and the nature of our Self, determines the fate that awaits us. If we believe and realize ourselves as ontologically identical with the transcendent reality, then we definitely become one with that reality by getting rid of the cosmic illusion. However, if we believe ourselves as belonging to the realm of phenomena, always subject to change, origin and decay, that precisely becomes the fate awaiting us in terms of our experiences. However, there is no doubt that the nature of reality is not at all affected by our right or wrong perception of it. At the same time, it is also true that our correct or incorrect understanding of reality definitely leads to corresponding experiences. Therefore, the wise ones do not believe in the magical show presented by the cosmic projective principle. They know that only the magician is real, while the magical show presented at the phenomenal plane is quite illusory. They take the creative principle and the supreme reality alone to be the real ontological grounds for the epistemic projection of the dualistic world. Realizing thus, they do not get embroiled in the magical show of spatio-temporal duality. On the other hand, the people who believe in the reality of the magical show and overlook the magician responsible for that, face the definite fate of suffering through the phenomenal cycle of transmigrations.

The eighty-third stanza[67] of the Śabda chapter points out that the supreme reality manifests itself at the physical plane in the form of each and every breath, producing the subtle vibration representing the vibration of the transcendent reality. The spiritually ignorant people do not know this fact and they are oblivious of the immanent nature of that supreme reality. This also indicates the importance of understanding the manifestation of that supreme vibration within our physiological constitution and its clear awareness is a very important means of spiritual realization.

In the ninety-fourth stanza[68] of the Śabda chapter Kabīra points out the inexpressibility of the nature of immutable and absolute reality. It does not have any characteristic. It is beyond all change. It does not have any form. It does not have any name. In that situation how can one possibly express it? How can one perform *japa* with respect to that supreme reality? Kabīra goes on to say that even Brahmā, the author of the four Vedas, is incapable of describing the nature and manifestations of that immutable reality. In spite of all this, that reality remains realizable at the intuitive plane. Therefore, Kabīra cajoles all persons desirous of liberation to strive for the inner intuitive realization of that reality alone. It is not a matter of linguistic expression or theoretical understanding.

In the one hundred and first stanza[69] of the Śabda chapter Kabīra says that the realization of supreme reality is truly amazing. There are very few people who have the exalted realization of the supreme reality. He says that in the state of this realization the earth merges into the space. This description refers to the involution of the various cosmic elements in the reverse order, e.g., the earth merging into water, then water into fire, and so on till they all merge back into space. In this manner the great expanse of the phenomenal universe is perceived to be merging back into the subtle causes one by one. This is the process through which a person gains an intuitive insight into the supreme uncaused cause and it is a truly wonderful process.

In the one hundred and eleventh stanza[70] of the Śabda chapter Kabīra says that the process through which the nature of reality seems to be appearing in an exactly opposite manner, is very wonderful. That which is the immutable, presents itself as the world of mutable phenomena. That which is the ocean of infinite bliss, appears as the realm of perennial suffering. This appearance in the opposite manner is possible only through the cosmic projective principle, the inalienable power of the supreme reality. Kabīra says that those who are cognizant of the phenomenal plurality, do not witness the true nature of the supreme reality. On the other hand, only those who are oblivious of the phenomenal manifestations, get an intuitive insight into the nature of reality. It is as if only those who are blind, are truly capable of seeing. This wonderous scenario is not comprehensible to people reposing their faith in logic and rationality.

In the one hundred and fifteenth stanza[71] of the Śabda chapter Kabīra says that the nature of the phenomenal universe is a network of epistemic imaginations. Being situated in the world immediately leads one to entanglement in the web of various epistemically projected principles. It is not possible to get rid of this web of epistemic illusions through any exercise executed at the plane of phenomenal logic and rationality. The only possible way out is by coming into contact with some spiritually realized soul, a competent preceptor or *Guru*. He alone has the capacity to guide one to the level of the highest intuitive realization, thus effecting freedom from the realm of epistemic illusions. All illusions and imaginations can be dissolved only by the medicine of direct intuitive realization. Any amount of conceptual deliberation is inherently incapable of eradicating the cosmic illusion. Only the direct intuitive realization of the supreme reality has the capacity to effect it.

The twelfth stanza[72] of the Jñāna Caumtīsā chapter points out that it is absolutely futile to run after various phenomena. Instead, one should strive to focus one's mind on the realm which is beyond all the phenomena. That is the realm which is the basis of everything. It is the ontological absolute and the transcendent reality. The intuitive realization of this reality alone is the way out of this cosmic illusion.

The sixteenth stanza[73] of the Jñāna Caumtīsā says that it is utterly futile to look for the supreme reality in the external sphere. One may go on searching endlessly for that reality in the phenomenal realm but it can never be revealed there. The reason is that the supreme reality manifests most clearly within our own consciousness and therefore it is the introspective meditation alone which can provide us the realization of that supreme reality.

The twenty-sixth stanza[74] of the Jñāna Caumtīsā chapter points out the pervasive nature of the cosmic illusion. Kabīra says that it is on account of this illusion that the thing which is truly our innermost nature and our Self, appears to be the most distant reality, in search of which we go on wandering from place to place endlessly. It is on account of this illusion that the illusion of phenomenal transmigration of the Self is experienced repeatedly. The way out of this is to look inwards to witness the inner manifestation of that supreme reality within our consciousness. The moment one attains an intuitive realization of the immanence and absoluteness of that reality, one is finally redeemed from the web of cosmic illusion.

In the twelfth stanza[75] of the Vipramatīsī chapter Kabīra says that the supreme creator has produced the entire world out of a common substance, just as a potter creates numerous pots out of the same clay. The same immutable vibration gets projected in the form of the entire phenomenal realm with the help of the primordial creative principle.

In the thirteenth stanza[76] of the Vipramatīsī chapter Kabīra says that it is the same transcendent light of consciousness which permeates the entire universe and it is a great folly to give it different names and distinguish between the various manifestations of that one reality in a substantive manner. Anyone practising such distinctions is actually going opposite to the nature of that transcendent reality and in that sense, it is virtually a demonic activity. Even the persons who are considered wise in the phenomenal, go on doubting the truth of that transcendent reality and they strive to prove or disprove it with the help of rational arguments and all this amounts to a demonic activity.

The opening line of the first stanza[77] of the Kaharā chapter says that the cosmic projective principle is the inalienable power of the supreme reality and despite that it is responsible for the phenomenal illusion. The line says that this creative principle is playing a kind of sport with all the beings in the phenomenal realm and She is utterly unattached to all the beings in her sport. Everyone at the phenomenal plane has to go through the same miserable cycle of transmigration, unless and until one has intuitively realized that transcendent reality.

The first line of the first stanza[78] of the Vasanta chapter points out that the supreme reality appears to be constantly enjoying the spring season in which there is a natural state of bliss of the highest order. There are very few people who actually witness the infinitely blissful nature of that supreme reality through their intuitive realization. Further, those who have such realization also partake of that supreme bliss in their superconscious meditative state of the mind.

The fourth line of the same stanza[79] says that once a qualified preceptor has pointed out the supreme reality to the disciple, one should take utmost care not to lose hold of it. Anyone who develops an intense desire to witness and enjoy the bliss of the transcendent reality, certainly comes to enjoy it in the due course of time, at the appropriate level of spiritual development.

The first stanza of the Cācara chapter[80] points out that the creative principle, which is the inalienable power of the supreme reality, plays a sort of divine sport in which all the beings of the phenomenal realm have become subjects. She is enjoying herself in various manners. Even the three principal cosmic deities - Brahmā, Viṣṇu and Maheśa - are not totally devoid of her bewitchment. They also fall prey to the illusion thrown up by her. Kabīra says that only those who are truly unattached to the phenomenal world of duality, those who are true renunciants, can hope to be free from the magic of that creative principle.

In the first stanza of the Belī chapter[81] Kabīra points out that the microcosmic manifestation of that divine reality, referred to as *'haṁsa'*, is residing in the physical body itself. However, we are not usually aware of its divine presence. It is a great wonder that despite our wakeful eyes, the illusion of duality has bewitched us and we are totally unaware of our sad plight. Kabīra says that those persons, who have acquired realization of that divine presence within themselves, become free from the illusion of duality. On the other hand, those who are not similarly awake to the non-dual reality, go on incessantly suffering in the phenomenal cycle of transmigration.

In the first line of the Birahulī chapter[82] Kabīra says that this transcendent reality is devoid of any beginning or end, which is to say that it is infinite and eternal. At the same time, it is an immutable reality. There are no divisions within it. There may be appearances taking place over this reality in the epistemic sense, even while there is no ontological division within this immutable absolute.

The second stanza of the Hiṁḍolā chapter[83] says that the creator has presented the world in the form of a cosmic entertainment. All the beings at the phenomenal plane are naturally attracted towards it for enjoying it. There are very few people who can restrain themselves from its temptations. Only such few people are the fortunate ones who can get rid of the cosmic illusion, coming to them in the form of great dualistic enjoyments.

In the fourth stanza of the Sākhī chapter[84] Kabīra points out very significantly that even the sacred Vedic texts are virtually blind without the guidance of intuitive realization in the form of the transcendent vibration. That is to say, without that *anāhata śabda,* even the śrutis are blind. The śrutis are the material manifestations of that transcendent vibration only and their ultimate goal is to guide us to that transcendent *anāhata śabda* only. Therefore, realization alone is the highest objective pointed out by the śrutis.

In the twenty-seventh stanza[85] Kabīra says that within the five elements constituting our physical body, there lies a secret treasure. However, very few people know about this secret treasure. The only way to know about it and actually obtain it, are the authoritative words of the realized preceptor.

In the thirty-fifth stanza[86] Kabīra says that people are very often talking about that transcendent reality, the *anāhata śabda,* but the fact is that the transcendent reality and vibration is without any form. There is no space and time to serve as its reference and therefore there can be no possibility of conceptually comprehending and linguistically expressing it. Despite this, people are always seen to be discussing it and this is an amazing situation. Kabīra says that the transcendent reality and its microcosmic manifestation is only a matter of direct intuitive realization, direct cognition. There is no possibility of arguing over it, describing it or even conceptualizing it.

In the sixty-ninth stanza[87] Kabīra says that people quite easily understand that the individual things are all situated within the universal reality. It is comprehensible to the phenomenal intellect. However, there is another aspect of the same reality. It is that the same universal reality is also microcosmically present within each particle constituting it. This is to say that the macrocosm is present within the microcosm as well, as if the whole ocean is represented in all its detail in each and every drop constituting it. However, such necessary representation of the macrocosm in the microcosm is realized by very few people and they are the ones who successfully overcome the cosmic illusion of plurality.

Later on, Kabīra says[88] that the one and only supreme reality is permeating the entire phenomenal universe. At the same time, the whole phenomenal universe is also located in that same supreme reality. Thus, the supreme reality is immanent in the phenomenal universe and the phenomenal universe is also situated within that same reality. Kabīra says that true bliss and liberation consist only in the intuitive realization of the non-duality of reality.

In the very next stanza[89] Kabīra says that those who understand the supreme importance of attaining spiritual realization succeed in obtaining all ends life in a very natural manner. They have access to real bliss and satisfaction. On the other hand, people who are hankering after infinite number of phenomenal desires and satisfactions are never successful in achieving true bliss and satisfaction. He gives the example of a tree. The person giving water to the roots of a tree manages to nourish each and every corner of that tree. On the other hand, a person sprinkling water upon only some particular branch or flower of that tree, will not be successful in nourishing the tree at all. Similarly, people who are focusing upon spiritual realization attain the highest bliss directly from that ultimate cause of the world. As such, that bliss manifests in each and every aspect of even their phenomenal life. However, those who are instead focusing upon phenomenal desires are bound to go through the cycle of frustration and suffering.

Kabīra further says[90] that the supreme reality does not have any colour or form. It has not taken the form of any particular body. Therefore, it can never be realized as a spatial and temporal entity. It can be realized only in the void of internal meditative space. There alone the transcendent light of consciousness manifests itself and reveals itself as the absolute and immutable reality.

At the end of the Sākhī chapter[91] Kabīra points out that people say that the supreme reality is beyond all cognition, but actually for the person having the highest intuitive realization, that very same reality is seen manifesting itself in each and every particle of the phenomenal universe. To that realized soul, the entire universe is but a manifestation of the supreme reality itself. He sees it everywhere. In that situation the description of that reality as transcendent and lying beyond all possibilities of cognition seems somewhat inappropriate. Kabīra says that those who do not have realization of the immanent nature of that supreme reality, have merely taken up the garb of realized persons. In fact, they are only misleading the worldly people.

On the basis of these selective passages from the Bījaka, it can be easily seen that Kabīra's realization convinced him that the supreme reality is immutable and non-dual in nature. At the same time, this reality is characterized by its inalienable potency or *śakti* which is responsible for the epistemic projection of the universe over the ontological reality of that supreme Brahman. This cosmic principle is responsible for all phenomenal projections of duality. Kabīra says that instead of getting bewitched by the cosmic play of duality, along with its associated desires and temptations, one should always strive for the highest spiritual realization by practicing meditation and trying to understand one's own true nature. He says that the same supreme reality, which is upholding the entire universe, is also equally manifest within each one of us and therefore, the right understanding of our own nature is equivalent to understanding the nature of that supreme reality. Such intuitive realization is the only thing necessary for transcending the realm of cosmic illusions. As such, the supreme reality, according to Kabīra, is manifest everywhere. It is immanent everywhere. At the same time, it is transcendent to the entire phenomenal realm as well. Thus, according to Kabīra, the nature of reality is definitely non-dual, but there is room for epistemic duality within it as well. It is definitely transcendent to the phenomenal realm, but it is universally immanent in it as well. That reality is definitely infinitely blissful, yet it also manifests itself as the realm of transmigration and suffering with respect to the ignorant *jīvas*. According to Kabīra, it is the spiritual obligation of all the *jīvas* to strive and realize the transcendent, non-dual and blissful nature of that reality and go beyond the cycle of phenomenal suffering.

Chapter III

Spiritual Ignorance and Existential Bondage

The discussion of spiritual ignorance *(avidyā)* and the resultant existential bondage holds a pre-eminent position in all schools of Indian philosophy. Even the individual saints of various orders, as well as mystics belonging to no explicit religious order, concede directly or indirectly, the phenomenal and existential problem of ignorance and bondage.

This problem has numerous dimensions. First of all, the nature of bondage and its means of ascertainment have to be decided. At least, the explicit symptoms of bondage need to be recognized. At the same time, the concept of bondage cannot be significant without referring to its subject. The genesis, process and resultant consequences of bondage also must be comprehended clearly.

Further, it is important to understand the nature of relationship between bondage and ignorance. It is pertinent to note whether it is a case of synonymous use of terms or whether it signifies a causal relationship. Or, are they simply two facets of the same concept and reality? Most importantly, one has to ponder over the point that if the subject and nature of bondage and ignorance may be possibly referring to some reality transcending the phenomenal plane of existence, then would it be logically consistent to assume that there should be and can be a perfect way of understanding it in terms of the spatio-temporal logic, language and rationality of the phenomenal plane. Obviously, the answers may not be simple and straight forward.

Moreover, there may be different levels of ignorance as well as bondage. It is possible that various subjects may be undergoing different levels of them at the same point of time or the same subject may be experiencing those different levels at different points of time. In such a situation it is extremely important to understand what could be the possible determining criteria for all this. Moreover, it would be worthwhile to see if there is any fixed sequential order in experiencing the various levels of bondage and ignorance.

Now, Kabīra was not a formal philosopher. Therefore, he had not proposed any rigorous conceptual framework for explaining the nature of reality, ignorance, bondage, knowledge, liberation, etc. However, he illustrated an eclectic synthesis of the various prominent schools of thought of his times, the core of which always remained his plane common sense and mystical intuitive insights. He never allowed any kind of orthodoxy and superstition to overwhelm the spiritual picture of reality emerging out of his intuitive experiences. He was very clear about the fundamental impossibility of explaining the nature of the highest reality in terms of phenomenal concepts and language, yet he was also acutely aware of the inevitability of doing exactly that for the sake of phenomenally bound people since they do not have a well-developed intuitive faculty to begin with. That is why again and again one can find various instances of apparently conflicting statements coming from Kabīra. In this chapter I will take a selective look at various passages from Kabīra's Bījaka so as to bring out his understanding of the nature, genesis, process, symptoms and consequences of ignorance and bondage.

In the very beginning of the Bījaka Kabīra clearly brings out the mere conventional and artificial nature of various religion-based practices.[92] He refers to the practices of both the Hindus and the Muslims to prove his point. He points out that the so-called divinity of the Brahmin caste is nothing pertaining to their inner nature. In fact, even their knowledge of the Vedas is but a phenomenally acquired skill only. Even the people of other lower castes are equally capable of learning them if they are given the right opportunities. Referring to the Muslims, he says that their religious practice of circumcision has been wrongly ascribed such great divine connotations since it is done only at the phenomenal plane and that too with respect to the physical body. Kabīra is thus eager to point out that the true essence of religion and spirituality lies primarily at the level of inner realizations only.

In the very next line of the same passage[93] Kabīra refers to basic cause of bondage and ignorance. It has both its individual and cosmic aspects. He uses the word *'nārī'*, meaning woman. It refers to the cosmic *Māyā* as the source of all the epistemic projections of phenomenal duality, including the phenomenal birth of various individual souls inhabiting different material bodies. In the individual context, this term refers to the attachment of one's mind to various material pleasures in the previous births, which is directly responsible for one's present existence at the phenomenal plane. The most prominent among these degrading material pleasures are those of sex and wealth i.e., *kāminī-kañcana*. Since the transmigratory cycle is believed to be beginningless, it follows that effectively the direct and immediate cause of bondage is nothing but one's intense desire and attachment for worldly pleasures.

Kabīra goes on to say that it is the one and same cosmic projective principle, *Māyā,* that has epistemically brought about the entire phenomenal realm over the absolute and immutable ontological reality of the highest Brahman.[94] Therefore, despite the phenomenal appearance of plurality, one needs to understand its misleading and illusory nature. As such, all sorts of phenomenal knowledge turn out to be ultimately misleading since they are based in the notions of plurality of phenomena. Kabīra, therefore, wonders as to how the worldly people treat such misleading concepts as cases of knowledge at all.

Kabīra goes on to show the vicious nature of the cycle of transmigration.[95] He says that due to one's attachment to the worldly pleasures, especially sex and wealth, one is compelled by the karmic force to take birth at the phenomenal plane. However, when one comes to the phenomenal plane one starts to once again indulge in the various material pleasures. As such, that fresh karmic indulgence becomes the grounds for the further bondage of the soul in future births. Thus, the desire for material enjoyments begets the circumstances for their enjoyment, whereas the enjoyment of material pleasures begets the desire for more such future enjoyment. The fact is that both the desire and enjoyment of material pleasures are but rooted in the notions of plurality, which is fundamentally misleading in the spiritual and ontological contexts. Thus, ignorance *(avidyā)* of the true nature of one's self and reality in general, is the primary cause of the phenomenal bondage of the soul, manifesting in the form of an endless transmigratory cycle of material enjoyments and their cravings.

Kabīra goes on to emphatically declare that all the forms and dealings of the phenomenal realm are ultimately misleading and illusory.[96] Those who live at the level of phenomenal appearances, by believing in them, are bound to be doomed. They have to go on facing the cycle of transmigrations. Their fate is sealed on account of their ignorance of the absolute and immutable nature of the highest reality, which is not different from their own Self. However, this ignorance must to be removed by an inner intuitive realization only. Any amount of intellectual and conceptual knowledge is inherently incapable of achieving that end since they are all based in the illusory notion of plurality.

Kabīra says that the epistemically projected realm of phenomenal plurality consists of both the spiritually oriented and the materially oriented people.[97] Both kinds of people are interested in understanding the nature of reality. However, whereas the spiritually minded people take the route of intuitive realizations for understanding the highest reality, the materially minded people repose their faith in the capabilities of logic, language and rationality. The spiritual people understand the absolute, infinite and inexpressible nature of that reality on the basis of their intuitive realizations, but the worldly people are mistaken in their prior assumption of the linguistic expressibility and logical comprehensibility of the nature of the highest reality. As opposed to the spiritual people who know the impossibility of grasping that reality in its entirety, the worldly people naively believe that it can be grasped in its completeness. Such enhanced and uncritical faith in capacities of our language and rationality is a mark of one's spiritual ignorance and bondage.

Kabīra says that the cosmic epistemic principle, *Māyā,* makes the bound people believe in the dualistic appearances of the phenomenal world and thus prompts them to perform various worldly and religious actions.[98] All such actions are rooted in the notion of phenomenal plurality. Further, these actions are always directed towards attaining some specific goals, believed to be different from the agent of those actions. Both the grounds and the objectives of these actions are based in the concept of plurality. Sometimes these actions are performed for the purpose of attaining gross material objectives, but at other times they are performed for attaining various duality based religious and spiritual ends. Nonetheless, both these kinds of actions are manifestations of the basic spiritual ignorance and thus they lead to the continuation of the soul's bondage.

Kabīra further describes the fate of the spiritually unrealized persons and contrasts it with that of the realized ones.[99] Those who have attained the inner realization of the highest reality get relief from the snare of the cosmic *Māyā*. Though continuing to exist at the phenomenal plane as a *jīvanmukta* or 'liberated-while-alive' person, their minds and bodies become pure due to their spiritual realization. Their karma engendered bodies and minds lose their capacity of throwing them into the illusion of phenomenal plurality. On the other hand, the people bereft of such intuitive realization of the highest reality keep on being attracted towards various material pleasures, facing their eventually dreadful consequences. Kabīra compares them with the moths who fling themselves into the flame out of their fatal desire for light. Such is the pitiable plight of the worldly people.

Kabīra appreciates the enormous difficulties in overcoming the epistemically projected forms of duality.[100] The difficulty arises from the fact that a naive and uncritical belief in the pluralistic nature of the world and reality is a natural characteristic of phenomenal existence. All the spiritually unrealized persons naturally repose their faith in phenomenal logic, language and rationality. As such, it becomes very difficult for them to find the way to spiritual realization. Kabīra says, what to talk of the ordinary people, even the gods belonging to the celestial realms become easy victims of the illusory projections of *Māyā*. Thus, spiritual ignorance and bondage is so natural and universal to phenomenal existence *per se* that one is usually unaware of its presence altogether. It requires careful and sustained reflection to be clearly aware of its problematic existence and nature.

Kabīra goes on to discuss the nature and limitations of duality-based religions and spiritual practices.[101] He says that all the scriptural descriptions of the nature of the highest reality are based in notions of plurality and all the intellectual comprehensions too reflect the same presuppositions. The Vedas and the Koran equally belong to the realm of illusory dualities. The complexity of the religious precepts and practices is baffling to the ordinary people, yet they adhere to them since they are unaware of any better alternative. The religious and devotional practices of various traditions have been there in all the ages. However, all such duality-based precepts and practices are bound to fail in achieving the liberative intuitive realization, just as one can never carry one's goods in a badly torn bag.

Describing the state and fate of the spiritually ignorant persons, Kabīra says that they are always in a state of running here and there in the hope of attaining that which may give them lasting peace and happiness.[102] However, due to the constantly unsteady state of their minds they are never successful in obtaining the true spiritual medicine that may relieve them from their phenomenal misery and ignorance. Their spiritual ignorance makes them oblivious of the transcendent and immutable nature of their own Self and in this state of ignorance they run towards the burning hell of the cravings and gratifications of phenomenal pleasures. Kabīra says that if only they could steady their minds, they could easily attain the liberative intuitive knowledge of the Self. However, their sensory approach to the world restrains them from moving in the direction of spiritual realization.

Pointing out the importance of the spiritual preceptor or Guru, Kabīra says that it is only on account of not receiving the guidance of the realized preceptor that one remains enmeshed in the illusion of phenomenal plurality and its attendant problems.[103] That is, the words and spiritual guidance of the Guru definitely have the capacity of saving one from phenomenal quagmire, if only the concerned person accepts the guidance of the Guru in one's life. The realized preceptor is a veritable phenomenal manifestation of the highest reality, performing the task of providing others the necessary spiritual guidance for getting rid of the phenomenal illusion. Such true Gurus have existed in all the ages but the pity is that people often do not listen to their words. The fact is that one requires a sustained moral life and the elevating company of spiritual people to come to a mental state where one would truly pay heed to the words of the spiritual preceptor.

Kabīra indirectly brings out the illusory nature of entire realm of phenomenal plurality[104] by pointing out the absence of the various appearances of the phenomenal realm in the transcendent non-dual reality. The transcendent reality does not have room for any kind of duality and distinction. Therefore, the entire realm of phenomenal plurality consisting of the various subtle and gross elements, the different sense-organs and their respective objects, the individual souls and the various bodies inhabited by them, as also the different bodies of worldly and spiritual knowledge, turn out to be ultimately illusory in nature due to their dualistic foundations. Nonetheless, it is also a fact that among all the things in the phenomenal realm, some of them are conducive to spiritual development, whereas most of them are detrimental to the spiritual life. But the fact remains that even the spiritually conducive phenomena can at best serve as mere stepping stones to the highest spiritual realization, which necessarily transcends the entire dualistic realm of phenomena.

Kabīra describes the different aspects of an individual soul's bondage at the phenomenal plane.[105] He says that the bound souls are fettered by nine ropes and they face an eight-fold misery. The nine fetters refer to the five-fold objects of the five sensory organs and the four-fold internal organs comprising of the mind *(manas)*, the intellect *(buddhi)*, the recollective faculty *(citta)* and the ego-principle *(ahaṁkāra)*. The eight miseries stand for the five-fold sufferings *(kleśas)* and the three constituent *guṇas* or energies of *Prakṛti*. The five sufferings are ignorance *(avidyā)*, ego-consciousness *(asmitā)*, attachment *(rāga)*, aversion *(dveṣa)* and clinging to the phenomenal existence *(abhiniveśa)*, whereas the three basic energies are *sattva*, *rajas* and *tamas*. Kabīra says that the cosmic epistemic projective principle, namely *Māyā*, projects the illusion of individuality before the soul and it thus ties it down to the phenomenal plane of suffering and mortality. He says that the entire phenomenal realm, without exception, is bound through the basic illusion of duality, as projected by cosmic *Māyā*.

Kabīra says that the sustained practice of spiritual disciplines is the only way to break the iron fetters of phenomenal bondage.[106] He says that the bonds of *Māyā* are so strong that even the gods belonging to celestial realms easily fall prey to it. But those who acquire faith in the words of the realized preceptors and subject themselves to their disciplines gradually move forward in the path of spiritual realization and eventually attain the highest intuitive realization in the transcendent fourth state or the *turīya-avasthā*.

Kabīra severely criticizes selfish devotion i.e., undertaking spiritual disciplines for the purpose of either acquiring phenomenal wealth and powers or getting rid of phenomenal afflictions.[107] He says people usually take to the practice of spiritual disciplines for selfish material objectives only. This is highly deplorable as such an objective immediately destroys the true spiritual potential of the disciplines. True spirituality should have only the aim of transcending the phenomenal realm of illusion by intuitively realizing the transcendent nature of the Self. Kabīra compares selfish devotion with the mere show of love by a woman for the purpose of acquiring wealth. Just as true love is never for the sake of amassing wealth, similarly true spirituality can never have the objective of winning phenomenal wealth and powers. Nonetheless, usually true love does bring in its fold wealth as well and similarly, even true spirituality does lead to acquiring various supernormal phenomenal powers in the due course of time. The deplorable element consists in having explicitly phenomenal goals as the aim of spiritual practices. However, Kabīra finds that most of the so-called spiritual people in the world are engaged in this kind of activity only. Such spirituality is just a pathetic manifestation of one's ignorance and bondage.

Kabīra says those who undertake spiritual practices for the sake of phenomenal benefits may happen to get their cherished objectives in the due course of time.[108] Obviously, such selfish devotion can never bring about the highest spiritual realization. For such a realization one needs to completely overcome the desire for the pleasures of the phenomenal realm. One must have true mental renunciation of all phenomenal pleasures. It is true mental renunciation, and not the mere outward show of renunciation, that is vital for the possibility of achieving the highest intuitive realization.

Discussing the essential nature of bondage and liberation, Kabīra says the world is totally engrossed in the enjoyment and pursuit of phenomenal pleasures.[109] The worldly people are in such a state of bondage on account of their ignorance of the transcendent blissful nature of their very own Self, which is identical with the highest reality as well. Kabīra clearly says that for those people who have overcome their desire for phenomenal experiences there is no further birth and death. That is, they easily and surely transcend the cycle of transmigration. However, there are two distinct stages of overcoming all phenomenal desires. In the pre-realizational stage of spiritual practices, one deliberately overcomes his phenomenal desires for the sake of spiritual realization on the advice of his spiritual preceptor. This paves the way for the highest spiritual realization. However, after intuitively experiencing the infinite bliss of the transcendent reality, the realized person finds all his deliberately suppressed phenomenal desires effortlessly annihilated since the greatest phenomenal pleasure turns out to be insignificant when compared to the infinite and unconditional bliss of the transcendent reality.

Kabīra expresses his amazement at the perplexing nature of the magical show of *Māyā* in the phenomenal realm.[110] He says that the state of affairs in the phenomenal realm is as if the cat and mouse are living together or as if an elephant is eating up a lion. This comparison is meant to show that even though the soul is inherently and eternally the immutable pure consciousness and bliss, it is seen to be taking itself as a mortal and suffering phenomenal being who is always in search of bliss. It is as if the ocean is looking for water in the ponds and wells. This impossible situation is the cosmic illusion projected by *Māyā*. The sensory picture of the world of duality is what the soul mistakenly takes to be true and all this becomes possible on account of its ignorance of the true nature of the Self. This is the nature of ignorance and bondage in the world.

Discussing the nature of the soul with respect to the experiences of bliss and misery, Kabīra says that just as a flower cannot bear even the slightest burden because of its delicate nature, similarly the soul, being essentially blissful in nature, is inherently incapable of adjusting itself to the slightest sense of misery and suffering.[111] Despite the inevitable phenomenal experiences of various kinds and degrees of misery in the world, the people are never at peace with the given nature of the world. They are always in search of ways and means of eradicating it and finding the way to a lasting peace and happiness. However, because of their restricted sensory outlook to the nature of reality and the Self, their search for peace and happiness is always in the sphere of external phenomenal world. Their efforts do lead to various phenomenal objects of convenience and enjoyment. However, the hope of finding lasting peace and happiness through them always falls flat. The simple reason for this is that the projected world of duality is inherently an antithesis to the true ontological nature of the Self viz. eternal, immutable and infinite bliss. Not knowing the true nature of the Self alone is the root cause of all miseries in the world. As long as this ignorance continues, the amassing of phenomenal objects of enjoyment only leads to even more novel varieties of suffering in the world, just as a blanket rapidly becomes heavy on absorbing water. Just as a blanket by itself is not so heavy but its coming into contact with water makes it immensely heavy and difficult to handle, similarly even though the soul is basically bliss *per se* the ignorance of its own nature makes the life of people in the phenomenal realm difficult to bear.

Discussing the plight of the worldly-minded people, Kabīra points out that they do not pay heed to the words of the revealed texts or the realized saints.[112] The reason for this is that they repose their complete faith in the phenomenal logic, language and rationality on the basis of their sensory outlook to the world. In this scheme of things, the non-sensory and intuitive way of understanding reality is never given due consideration by them. On the contrary, despite knowing in a sure manner that all rational and linguistic understanding of things are incomplete and full of discrepancies, they go on exerting themselves in the pursuit of phenomenal kind of knowledge only. However, such knowledge does not save them from their phenomenal fate of mortality, suffering and transmigration. Kabīra says the untamed wild animal of the form of perennial doubt always vitiates their minds because of which they are not able to move towards the goal of spiritual realization. In their state of spiritual ignorance, they lose their most invaluable gift i.e., the knowledge of the transcendent and blissful nature of the Self.

Kabīra then points out the nature of the uncontrolled mind.[113] He says that the mind always keeps on throwing the forms of various imagined objects and experiences before the Self and thus the Self remains deluded by it. Although the basic nature of the mind is nothing but pure consciousness only, that consciousness keeps on temporarily projecting various forms, just as the ocean keeps on throwing various forms of waves on its surface. The formless mass of water in the ocean alone is the basic reality, whereas its various waves are mere passing forms appearing before the spectator. The spatio-temporal forms of various phenomenal objects are presented by the mind before the Self due to the cosmic play of *Māyā*. It is a ceaseless operation. This projective play takes place over the immutable ontological reality of the Self, which is just the same as the highest Brahman.

Pointing out the miserable nature of the phenomenal realm, Kabīra says that the worldly existence is full of miseries.[114] There is no end to the possible sufferings in the world. The only way to save oneself is by resorting to the name of Rāma i.e., by earnestly taking up spiritual disciplines in the guidance of some realized preceptor. Only those who have attained the highest intuitive realization can overcome the projective illusions of *Māyā* even while remaining at the phenomenal plane of existence. Kabīra says that the worldly people become so egotistic on acquiring even little phenomenal wealth that they completely become oblivious of their inevitable mortality at the phenomenal plane. Even so, when death starts staring into their faces in old age and diseases, they easily lose their mental composure. It is usually at fag end of their lives that they realize the utter futility of all phenomenal pursuits. It is as if they had been happily eating poison throughout their lives believing it to be nectar.

Kabīra points out the fatal and illusory nature of all phenomenal pleasures by giving the example of the moth and the burning flame.[115] The moth is unaware of the fact that the light which seems so dear to it, is actually a place of burning heat that is quite fatal. In its ignorance of its fatal heat and the overpowering attraction of its light, the moth rushes towards the flame and meets its horrific death. In a similar manner, the worldly people are immediately attracted towards various phenomenal objects and experiences in the belief that they will derive lasting peace and happiness out of it, but all this is a false hope. Nevertheless, the fact remains that all the people in the world are ontologically one with the transcendent blissful reality and therefore, despite their prevailing ignorance of their true nature, they always feel the inner urge to look for a lasting happiness. They are mistaken in their search only so far as they try to find it in the external phenomenal sphere. Further, the reason why the various phenomena appear to be sources of bliss and happiness is that the entire phenomenal realm too is an epistemic projection effected by *Māyā* over the non-dual blissful ontological reality. As such, despite the illusory appearance of plurality in the world, the basically blissful nature of reality is able to manifest itself in a very limited manner at the level of various phenomena. Even that limited manifestation of bliss is sufficient to overpower the worldly people thirsting in search of a lasting bliss and happiness. However, all the appearances of phenomena necessarily involve the basic ignorance of the Self, which is the same as the transcendent reality and this ignorance ensures that there can be no possibility of a lasting bliss in any phenomena *per se*. The primary ignorance of duality rules out the simultaneous possibility of realizing the immutable bliss of the Self. Therefore, the worldly people always suffer ultimately even while striving to find lasting happiness in the sphere of phenomenal objects and experiences. Kabīra therefore exhorts the worldly people to closely reflect over the nature of the phenomenal realm so that they may save themselves from the facade of worldly happiness and then begin their search for the highest bliss.

Criticizing the so-called preceptors, who are actually devoid of true inner realization, Kabīra says that they lead their followers into developing a superstitious faith in their words.[116] They preach about the absolute unreality of the four stages of life and the world in general but the fact is that they just talk big and befool the masses. Kabīra says that if the world were absolutely unreal then they should not have made any effort to even remain alive at the phenomenal plane, leave alone enjoying it in any manner. But this is never the case. They talk of spiritual merit and demerit but they have no realization at all. Without true realization one cannot know the nature of the Self, the world and the higher reality. In such a situation all spiritual preaching turn out to be a mere play of words. An unrealized person can never lead others to realization. True realization cannot be attained through any amount of verbal and intellectual exercise. Only those who are able to come out of the web of language and its involved rationality can have an access to the inner realization of the transcendent nature of the Self.

Pointing out the illusory potential of language, Kabīra says that it is capable of formulating various names which are supposed to refer to various things, distinct from one another.[117] This creates the illusion of plurality where there is none. An apodeictic faith in the referential capacity and nature of language, especially names, is one of the basic forms of illusions characterizing the phenomenal realm. The illusion of plurality, deriving from the basic nature of language, fortifies the basic ignorance of the non-dual nature of the reality and the Self. This results in the continuous suffering of going through the cycle of transmigration.

Discussing the nature of the six important philosophical systems and the Vedas, Kabīra brings out the fundamental difference between the texts of philosophy and those of revelations.[118] He says that all the philosophical systems are full of verbal jargons and empty intellectual argumentations. Each one of them has its own prior commitments to uphold and for this purpose they are more interested in the logical demolition of the viewpoint of other philosophical systems. In their zest to play with words and concepts and to prove their superiority with respect to the other systems, they have lost track of the nature of reality and the Self as well. In contrast to the texts of philosophy, the revealed texts, such as the Vedas, merely present the various aspects of the highest reality, including its manifestations at the phenomenal plane. They do not try to work out a logical framework out of these various aspects of reality with the help of arguments and criticism. They have no presupposition requiring them to believe that the nature of even the highest reality must conform to the dictates of the phenomenal logic, language and rationality. That is why the revealed texts merely proclaim the wondrous and varied aspects of the ultimate reality and also remain completely mute when it comes to its positive linguistic description. The silence of the revealed texts eloquently speaks about the inexpressible and only intuitively realizable nature of the highest reality.

Pointing out the paramount importance of the intuitive realization of the transcendent nature of the Self, Kabīra says that the study of Smṛtis and Vedas is futile if the person does not have an inner realization.[119] He says mere theoretical knowledge of the various scriptures often leads to a sense of inflated egoism. Such people take themselves to be great knowers of reality but they only indulge in various deplorable activities, e.g., the sacrifice of animals in the name of pleasing various deities, the practice of inhuman discriminations in the name of caste and religion, etc. Since these people lack the intuitive realization of the transcendent reality it is but natural that their behaviour with the surrounding people and beings does not reflect the love, knowledge and modesty of a realized person. They practise hypocrisy in the name of religion, philosophy and spirituality.

Kabīra discusses the hopeless situation of the ignorant people who do not have the benefit of the guidance and company of spiritually realized saints.[120] He says just as a mirror is incapable of showing a blind person his own image, similarly even the revealed texts, such as the Vedas, are incapable of helping a person immersed in worldly ideas and activities. Just as a spoon does not enjoy the taste of the nectar contained in it and the donkey does not enjoy and understand the value of the sandalwood it carries, similarly the persons engaged in the study and preaching of religious and spiritual texts do not derive any benefit from it without the company of spiritual people, which is necessary for relieving their minds from the varied worldly engagements. Kabīra says that they go on making huge speculations about the nature and deliberations of the highest reality but it is all in vain as they do not have the inner realization that is a *sine qua non* for the liquidation of one's egoism.

Kabīra is perplexed to see the egotistic and foolish efforts of many worldly people who strive to move ahead in the path of spiritual realization.[121] He says that without the guidance of the spiritually realized persons it is extremely difficult, uncertain and time consuming to try for spiritual realization. Without their guidance, despite the best efforts by the spiritual aspirants, a lot of effort may remain misdirected and thus may not give the desired results. Kabīra says that when the realized persons are available to them, then it makes more sense to directly benefit out of their experience instead of trying the hit and trial method according to one's imperfect understanding. He compares the situation to the case of a thirsty person who does not drink water directly from the well in front of him and instead starts digging a new well for quenching his thirst.

Kabīra shows that pride and egoism as absolutely contrary to the spiritual life of a person.[122] Pride of any variety only serves to inflate the sense of egoism for a person whether it relates to one's caste, wealth, education, gender, nationality, culture, religion or even spiritual status. He says too much of pride is totally unacceptable to God and that is why He is also known as the 'vanquisher of pride'. Only the meek and humble souls receive the blessings of God and spiritual personalities. Moreover, the control and eradication of all kinds of pride and egoism is, in its own right, a much-valued spiritual discipline as it is a yardstick for measuring one's spiritual progress.

Discussing the near universal sway of *kāma* or sexual attraction as a basic characteristic of the phenomenal realm,

Kabīra says that in this world it is a natural thing for the opposite sexes to be engrossed with one another.[123] Such attraction is one of the strongest bonds of *Māyā* and therefore overcoming it requires a lot of effort along with the support of spiritual company. Such attraction is rooted in the mistaken notion of one's identity in terms of gender and also in terms of the individual status of oneself *vis-à-vis* the other people. Kabīra says there are very few people who give up their sense of gender-based identity and see themselves as one with the highest *Puruṣa* or the transcendent and immutable reality.

Kabīra brings out the futility of running after the other all-pervasive bond of *Māyā* i.e., material wealth.[124] He says the life of phenomenal beings is so short and all the wealth has to be left in this world only at the time of death. No body can enjoy its benefits in the other worlds or in the next life. He refers to the legendary king Hariścandra who had immense wealth and says that even he is nowhere to be seen now. That is, the inevitable death of people living at the phenomenal plane makes pointless the amassing of too much wealth. Kabīra is amazed to see that the worldly people are engrossed in their money-making activities till their last breath, seemingly oblivious of their inevitable mortality as a phenomenal being. They express their condolence at the demise of their near and dear ones but never completely absorb the fate of their own inevitable mortality. Kabīra jokingly says that even while they may be on their death-beds they go on calculating the interest earned on their investments.

Kabīra severely criticizes all caste and religion-based distinctions and their attached notions of superiority and inferiority.[125] Pointing out the hypocritical sense of superiority so characteristic of the Brahmins, he says that if they were really superior to others in an inherent manner, then they should have been born with all the characteristic marks of an orthodox Brahmin. However, that is never seen to be the case. On the contrary, the scriptures pronounce that everybody is but a *Śūdra* at the time of his birth and death. He says all the ritualistic marks associated with the Brahmins are merely conventional matters with the express aim of making a religious business out of it. The physiological constitution of the Brahmins is no different from the people of other castes. Their process of birth is also just the same. Kabīra also talks of the Muslims and says that they too are equally wrong in believing themselves to be the most favoured ones in the eyes of God. The religious marks of the Muslims distinguishing them from the other religious communities, such as circumcision, too are just conventional and artificial in nature. They are not born with those distinguishing marks. Kabīra says whatever may be the colour of a cow, its milk is always only white in colour. The effort to draw distinctions between people in the name of caste and religion is akin to drawing distinctions between the milk of various cows according to the colours of those cows. He exhorts everybody to give up all these artificial distinctions between the people and see the one great reality manifesting in all of them in an equal manner.

Kabīra says that dancing and jumping in the name of devotion to God without the sense of inner realization is of no use for spiritual development.[126] They are mere outwardly exhibitions of spirituality and all for the sake of make-believe. Further, those who hurt other beings in any manner certainly cannot be having the inner realization of the universal immanence of the one and only supreme reality. Persons having true realization see their own Self in all the beings and as such they become instinctively merciful towards all the beings. Moreover, abiding truthfulness is one of the most important spiritual disciplines and therefore if a person's heart and tongue do not exhibit harmony, it can easily be taken as a sign of his gross material outlook. Such people do not have any chance of spiritual realization and they continuously go through the cycle of transmigration. Unless and until they realize and rectify their mistakes, they have no chance of escaping the cycle of phenomenal suffering. Kabīra also points out that those who go against the directions of their accepted spiritual preceptor or criticize them, have to face extremely bad karmic consequences, like being born as animals in their future lives. He says that the only way out of the phenomenal cycle of eighty-four lakhs kinds of births is through intuitively realizing the transcendent and yet universally immanent supreme reality as one's Self.

Kabīra condemns the violence and greed practised by the monks and renunciants of various religious sects.[127] He says he cannot remember the great sage Nārada having ever fired a gun or the great Vyāsa having ever beaten the battle-drum. He says only the spiritual morons indulge in violent activities. Those who indulge in violence cannot be true sages at all. He further says that it is quite comical to see the so called renunciants exhibiting intense greed and amassing material wealth. When such so called renunciants wear gold and other ornaments they verily insult their ochre robes. They are even seen to be having huge numbers of horses, etc. They take out gaudy processions on receiving vast tracts of lands and villages as charity from the kings.

They show the pride and egoism of millionaires. Such hypocrite renunciants go to the extent of having even female companions. Kabīra says the company of the opposite sex does not fit into the character of a true renunciant. He compares such company to an earthen pot blackened with soot which leaves its mark instantly on the hand touching it. That is, any kind of indulgence in violence, greed and sex does not fit in with the vows and character of a true saint and renunciant. Those behaving in the opposite manner are certainly hypocrites who give a bad name to the order of saints and renunciants.

Kabīra wonderfully points out the various claimants to the physical body of a person which is so instinctively taken to be one's own in the strictest sense of the term.[128] He says it is only after a long haul in the cycle of transmigration that one comes across the chance of acquiring a human body. It is an invaluable opportunity to strive for self-realization. The failure to make good use of it results in a very long wait for the next similar occasion. One should look at the human body as a rare spiritual opportunity and not as a means of phenomenal enjoyments. One should not be vainly egoistic about it. Further, it is not one's private property. There are numerous claimants of it. The parents claim it as their own and nourish it since childhood for their own largely selfish purposes. The wife loudly proclaims it as her own and holds on to it like a tigress. The children are always expecting various things from it even when the body starts wearing out in old age. Moreover, the dogs, crows and vultures look forward to the impending death of a person in the hope of getting their due shares in the dead body. The fire thinks it will burn and devour it, whereas the water thinks of drifting it away. The earth thinks it will merge into it and the air thinks it will have the opportunity of taking it away. Kabīra says that despite such a situation the worldly people behave like fools and treat their physical bodies as their real homes. The fact of the matter is that if the body is not engaged in spiritual pursuits then it proves to be just like an iron fetter in one's neck. However, the sad reality is that the vast majority of people in the world treat their bodies as a mere vehicle of material enjoyments and are extremely egotistic about it.

Kabīra presents a graphic description of the troublesome situation occurring in the mind and body of the worldly persons.[129] He compares it to a home in which an uncultured mother has continuous problems with her five greedy and obstinate sons. The foolish mother stands for the uncontrolled worldly mind and her five quarrelsome sons stand for the five sensory organs. Day and night they are fighting among themselves to have their own ways. All the five sons have a gluttonous appetite and taste and they are always demanding more and more, never to be satiated. That is, all the five sense organs are ever eager to enjoy more and more objects of sense experience. Their desires know no end. Kabīra says the way to end this perennial quarrel is to banish the foolish mother and strictly discipline the five unruly sons. That is, one must get rid of the worldly mentality with the help and guidance of the spiritual preceptor. Further, one must learn to discipline and control the berserk sense organs through the practice of necessary spiritual disciplines.

Kabīra presents the amazingly hypocritical plight of worldly people engaged in making a show of their religiosity.[130] He says that he finds the world going mad. The worldly people are quite happy to listen to lies but they run to hit if the truth of the world and the higher reality is put before them. He says he has seen so many so-called religious persons taking early morning baths but still practising the sacrifice of animals and the worship of stones. Verily, they cannot be supposed to have any spiritual knowledge at all. He says he has also come across many preachers of different religions who are quite busy with the study and teaching of their religious texts. They also have their disciples behind them but their egotism betrays their ignorance of the supreme reality. He says he has seen many people practising special yogic postures for a long time but all that only seems to enhance their sense of egotism. They are busy in the worship of stone and metal idols and they revel in the idea of having visited various places of pilgrimage. They put on various outer symbols and garbs to show off their religious identities and affiliations. They sing and recite the words of saints and revealed texts and yet they lack an inner realization of the supreme reality. Kabīra says both the Hindus and the Muslims proclaim the superiority of their own Gods and even fight and die in the name of God. Their berserk behaviour proves they have no inkling of the essence of spirituality. They are always so busy in increasing the numerical strength of their folds. But the fact remains that such worldly preceptors and their disciples are spiritually doomed and they have to repent their mistakes at the end of their lives. Kabīra persuades one and all to give up all these false exhibitions of religion and spirituality and take to the path of honesty, modesty, simplicity, self-control and renunciation. He says the supreme reality is rather simple *(sahaja)* and the simple people can easily attain it with the guidance of the realized spiritual preceptor.

Kabīra further says that it is because of the fact of not being successful in getting rid of the basic illusion of one's identity and nature that one has to repeatedly fall prey to the god of death.[131] He says what to talk of the worldly people who are always enmeshed in the ideas of distinctions and hierarchies, even the order of monks and renunciants is found to be bogged down with the same mentality. That is, the snare of illusory duality does not leave out even the vast majority of the spiritual people. Kabīra further says that without the attainment of intuitive realization of the supreme reality, the mere theoretical study of the Smṛtis and the Vedas is of no good. He compares it to the case of a person trying to change iron into gold by washing it again and again but the fact is that without the touch of the philosopher's stone it can never be so. Similarly, it is only the intuitive realization of the Self as being identical with the supreme reality that can truly save a person from the cycle of transmigration. Kabīra says that if a person does not achieve self-realization while being alive as a human being at the phenomenal plane, then there can be no possibility of that realization after the death either. It is so because it is only in the human body that there is the possibility of the highest spiritual realization. Not even the beings of the subtle celestial realms have that kind of opportunity. Moreover, what a person thinks and does throughout the greater part of his life is remembered at the time of death as well and the future course of the soul's spiritual journey is determined by the dominant thought at the time of physical death. Kabīra says it is necessary to take stock of all the good and bad actions performed by us throughout our lives, whether they were done knowingly or unknowingly. It is necessary because we have to face the consequences of all those actions sooner or later and further, by reflecting in this manner we can grasp the imperative need of transforming ourselves by giving up the material life of a bound and ignorant soul. But, Kabīra says, nobody can help a person if he insists on behaving like a blind person even while seeing the reality in a clear and crisp manner. The case of the worldly people is like that since even while witnessing the pathetic end of all material pursuits in the case of other persons they do not learn their lessons and think that it will be very different in their own particular case.

Kabīra says that the pundits indulging in intricate argumentations and technical jargons actually indulge themselves in mere false imaginations.[132] Neither theoretical discussions about the supreme reality nor the mere verbal repetition of God's name can ultimately save a person from phenomenal bondage. On the contrary, it only gives a false sense of satisfaction and boosts one's ego. The intuitive realization of the supreme reality alone is the necessary condition of freedom from the phenomenal bondage. Kabīra says that if the mere verbal repetition of the name of God is believed to be sufficient for freedom from ignorance and bondage then by just repeating the word 'sugar' the mouth should have been sweetened. He says that all the miseries of the world would have been easily solved if just by pronouncing the word 'fire' it would have been possible to burn something, or by pronouncing 'water' one's thirst would have been quenched, or by pronouncing 'food' one's hunger would have been satisfied. He further says that even a parrot repeats the name of God along with his master without understanding the greatness of God. But, if by chance the parrot happens to fly off into the jungle then it never remembers or repeats the name of God. Kabīra says that without the intimate vision and communion with that transcendent yet immanent supreme reality one cannot derive any spiritual benefit by merely repeating God's name in a mechanical manner. If by merely saying the word 'wealth' one could have become wealthy then nobody would have been poor in this world. Kabīra points out that the hard fact is that worldly people only love the phenomenal objects of pleasure and they often rush to punish the true devotees of God. Still, the fact remains that without the sincere practice of spiritual disciplines in the guidance of some realized saint there can be no hope of escape from the perennial cycle of phenomenal births and deaths.

Pointing out the importance of discrimination, renunciation and other spiritual disciplines, Kabīra says that without the regular practice of the necessary spiritual disciplines one cannot get rid of his worldly ways.[133] He says even after hearing the words of saints and the sacred texts the worldly people do not mend their ways. It is as if they have become blind by losing their eyes of wisdom and discrimination. Any amount of spiritual company cannot help those worldly persons who have not resolved in their hearts to strive for spiritual upliftment. Kabīra says one may immerse a stone in water for as long as one may wish but when it is taken out and struck against another stone it immediately starts throwing sparks. Pouring a thousand pitchers of water on a stone cannot make it really wet. It remains as dry as ever. Kabīra says that despite advancing age the worldly people remain young in their minds due to the excessive attachment to sensory pleasures. Even though their bodies get worn out, they go on imagining the varied sensory pleasures of the phenomenal objects in their minds. He says the yogis go on repeating the term 'anahada' without grasping its significance. They do not realize the absolute pervasion and immutability of the *anāhata śabda*. Kabīra finally says that only those who are fortunate enough to get the merciful guidance of a realized preceptor happen to enjoy the infinite bliss of the highest spiritual realization.

Thus, it can be seen that for Kabīra the genesis of phenomenal bondage lies in the ignorance of true nature of the Self, which is basically identical with the transcendent and yet universally immanent supreme non-dual reality. This ignorance is the result of both the cosmic *Māyā's* epistemic projections and the individual soul's past karmas at the phenomenal plane. This ignorance manifests itself as the characteristic pattern of thoughts and activities of worldly persons, always striving to acquire and enjoy more and more phenomenal pleasures. The accompanying bondage takes the form of the perennial cycle of transmigration for the individual soul, which always faces the fate of unfulfilled desires and its resultant frustrations. Kabīra says that such a pathetic state of the soul can come to an end only through the intuitive realization of the transcendent nature of the Self.

Chapter IV

Spiritual Enlightenment and Liberation

The attainment of spiritual enlightenment or self-realization *(ātma-jñāna)* and its resultant liberation *(mokṣa)* are the ultimate objectives for most of the religious and philosophical schools of Indian tradition. As such, all the other aspects of life are ideally designed to be in harmony with this objective. Despite this, there is no unanimity regarding either the basic nature or the various aspects of this knowledge and liberation.

The concept of knowledge has to be juxtaposed with that of its corresponding ignorance. Therefore, in the context of Indian religious and philosophical traditions both knowledge and ignorance refer to the spiritual sphere transcending the phenomenal realm. This is also clear from the spiritual context of bondage and liberation, which are directly related with the concepts of ignorance and knowledge respectively.

Given the transcendent spiritual context of knowledge and liberation, the question immediately arises as to what could be the possible role of phenomenal knowledge, comprising of sensory cognitions and rational understanding, with respect to that highest spiritual knowledge. The ordinary human beings are stationed at the level of phenomenal knowledge and therefore it is imperative for them to make a start from where they actually are. They do not have any other option.

On the other hand, it is also necessary to grasp the problems and limitations arising from the distinct levels of phenomenal and spiritual knowledge. Whereas the former is always in need of linguistic and conceptual articulation, the latter is not amenable to such articulation at all. Yet, it needs to be articulated in some manner or the other for the sake of the spiritually aspiring people. This is undoubtedly a formidable task, but it has been undertaken by numerous mystic-saints down the ages.

The nature of spiritual knowledge in terms of its genesis, faculty, validity, scope of application, benefits, etc. are the other issues of importance. It is also important to see if there are different levels of spiritual knowledge and if so, then what determines the experiential level of a given subject. One needs to understand the various phenomenal circumstances which may be conducive to or detrimental to the achievement of different levels of spiritual knowledge. One definitely needs to see if there are some external characteristics of attaining such spiritual knowledge and if there are, then what are the most common ones amongst them.

Further, it is most interesting to see what are the effects of gaining the highest spiritual knowledge. What is the internal and external state of such a realized person? In what sense may such a person feel oneself to be different from and existentially superior to the common people living at the plane of spiritual ignorance? In what sense can he claim to be liberated in comparison with the spiritually ignorant masses? Does such a realization make any difference to the nature of his continued phenomenal existence or is it entirely soteriological in nature? Is there any truly determinable highest spiritual realization, so to say? If yes, then what is it? If no, then what level of realization is a sufficient guarantee for liberation from the phenomenal bondage? Alternatively, what level of realization may be construed sufficient for negating the ignorance responsible for bondage?

All these questions and queries have a direct bearing on the discussion of knowledge and liberation. It is with reference to these various aspects that I will selectively refer to some of the passages of Kabīra's Bījaka for trying to get an insight into Kabīra's understanding of knowledge and liberation. However, we must always bear in mind that he was not even formally educated, leave alone being a formal philosopher, and therefore his discussions betray a ubiquitous experiential character.

In the very beginning of the Bījaka Kabīra points out the three important aspects of the nature of reality.[134] They are- (a) its transcendence, immutability and non-duality, (b) its eternal projective power, namely *Māyā* and (c) the inner light of consciousness i.e. the Self. The true realization of the highest reality must encompass all these three aspects of the reality. It is imperative to realize that the transcendent reality is the same as the universally immanent one. Also, the macrocosmic reality is not different from its microcosmic manifestation as the self of the individual being. Further, it is also important to realize that even though the epistemically projected phenomenal realm may not be independently real in the ontological sense, yet it is not absolutely illusory either, since the one and only transcendent and immutable reality alone constitutes its ontological essence and substratum. Similarly, the supreme realization must also reveal the fact that the cosmic projective principle responsible for the appearance of the phenomenal realm is but the inalienable projective power and nature of the supreme non-dual Brahman. The indisputable intuitive realization of all these aspects of the supreme reality is the sole means of transcending the realm of phenomenal illusions and sufferings. Such spiritual knowledge, however, is not achievable without the loving and merciful guidance of some realized preceptor.

Kabīra says that even though the world does have the appearance of a pluralistic realm, it is necessary to realize its illusory character.[135] He points out that the entire world is based in the same ontological reality and further, it is the same projective principle that is responsible for bringing forth the phenomenal realm in all its details and varieties. The whole world has the same cosmic father and mother. In such a situation any piece of phenomenal knowledge reflecting and assuming the pluralistic nature of the world can at best be treated as practically expedient at the phenomenal plane. Any phenomenal knowledge, being grounded in the notions of plurality, cannot be accepted as reflecting the nature of the supreme reality. In fact, it presents a picture quite opposite to the nature of the highest reality. Phenomenal knowledge is always based in logic, language, rationality and the evidence of the sense organs. As such, it is obvious that in order to gain an intimate knowledge of the Self, the supreme Brahman and the nature of the world, it is necessary to overcome the phenomenal limitations of logic, language, rationality and the sense organs. This supreme spiritual knowledge can be attained only through the regular practice of various spiritual disciplines with the help of a realized preceptor.

Kabīra refers to the linguistic inexpressibility of the knowledge derived through intuitive realization.[136] He says that infinite are the glories and deliberations of the supreme reality. It is beyond all change and activity and yet it alone is ultimately behind all the activities in the world. How far can anyone speak about it with a single tongue? Kabīra says it would require one to have a million tongues to attempt describing the nature of the supreme reality. That is, it is absolutely impossible for any phenomenal being to describe the complete nature of that supreme reality. The infinite vastness of that reality is one of the reasons for its indescribability. The other and more fundamental reason of its inexpressibility is that the supreme Brahman, being transcendent in its pure ontological nature, is categorically beyond the range of phenomenal concepts and language. It can only be realized intuitively. Any effort to express it in words and concepts is bound to present its distorted and imperfect picture only. That is why Kabīra says that any amount of study of even the revealed texts or listening to the words of the realized saints is utterly insufficient without one's own intuitive self-realization.

Kabīra emphatically declares the nature and benefit of the intuitive realization of the true nature of the Self and the supreme Brahman, while contrasting it with the case of various deliberations pertaining to the phenomenal realm.[137] He says that the entire phenomenal realm is a framework of epistemic projections grounded in the reality of the supreme non-dual Brahman. The various characteristic phenomenal parameters e.g., space, time, causality, change, names, plurality, etc. are misleading in the ultimate analysis. The sense and logic based phenomenal understanding and language presuppose and thus present the pluralistic picture of the world, which is quite opposite to the real nature of the supreme Brahman and the self. Therefore, Kabīra declares all phenomenal cases of knowledge to be illusory in the ultimate analysis. Such a misleading picture of reality is responsible for the phenomenal bondage of the individual soul, the *jīvātman*. Kabīra says that only the true intuitive knowledge of the supreme Brahman can save the *jīva* from the endless cycle of transmigration. The highest spiritual realization alone is the perfectly true knowledge.

He points out the nature of the self in the case of an individual living at the phenomenal plane.[138] He says that the inner light of consciousness in the case of phenomenal beings is directly rooted in the infinite consciousness of the supreme and non-dual Brahman. It is only the appearance of individuality of the *jīva* that is actually illusory, being epistemically projected by *Māyā*. Consciousness *per se* is never a case of illusion. Therefore, the liberative spiritual knowledge constitutes in having a direct and intuitive realization of the absolute, immutable and non-dual nature of one's consciousness i.e., the Self. Once the illusoriness of the sense of one's individuality is revealed intuitively the person gets immediately liberated from bondage to the phenomenal realm. In fact, liberation is not something to be attained in any ontological sense at all, since the sole ontological reality is immutable as well. Liberation is just a matter of perfectly realizing the transcendent and absolute nature of the Self, which is at once identical with the supreme non-dual Brahman. Liberation constitutes in just getting rid of the cosmic and beginningless ignorance by negating it with true spiritual realization.

Kabīra points out the reality which existed first of all and he also indicates the nature and origination of the phenomenal realm.[139] He says very simply that the reality which would have existed first of all, must also be the one responsible for bringing about everything else. That is, it must be accepted that the entire phenomenal realm must be having its genesis in the primordial reality. That which is responsible for producing the other, either in the ontological or the epistemic sense, must also be treated as the higher reality. According to Kabīra the phenomenal realm is the result of the epistemic projection effected by the cosmic *Māyā* over the ontological ground of the non-dual supreme Brahman. As such, there are two aspects of the genesis of the phenomenal realm, namely the ontological and the epistemic. However, the non-dual and transcendent nature of the source of the world implies that the ontological and epistemic aspects of the transcendent reality cannot be treated as being separate at all. They are one and the same, like the fire and its nature and power to burn. The ontologically immutable nature of the transcendent reality also implies the mere epistemic nature of the apparent pluralistic realm. The true liberative spiritual knowledge constitutes in intuitively realizing the ontologically absolute and immutable nature of the Self, along with the mere epistemic and illusory nature of all the ideas of plurality and change.

Highlighting the supreme value of the non-dual transcendent reality *vis-à-vis* the numerous other manifestations of godhead controlling the phenomenal realm, Kabīra says that he takes refuge only in the supreme and transcendent Brahman, the all-pervasive Rāma.[140] The reason for this is that he had seen the illusoriness of the entire dualistic realm, including the realm pertaining to the various gods. Being attached to any form of dualistic manifestation of the non-dual reality necessarily involves ignorance and that in turn ensures some measure of phenomenal bondage as well. The idea is that one can have liberation only through the perfect spiritual knowledge constituting of realizing the Self as being fundamentally identical with the non-dual and transcendent Brahman.

Kabīra points out the effect of the true spiritual realization.[141] Persons having such realization become *jīvanmukta-s* or the liberated-while-alive. They continue to live at the phenomenal plane due to the already fructifying force of their *prārabdha karmas*. They live until the full exhaustion of the *prārabdha karmas*. Although they appear to have a physical body and seem to be situated in the spatio-temporal phenomenal realm, the fact is that having realized once and forever the illusory nature of all duality, they know themselves only as the transcendent non-dual Brahman. For them, the phenomenal world is but a cosmic dream, the dream nature of which has already been exposed to them. In contrast to the realized persons, the worldly people are condemned, because of their ignorance, to lead the perennially frustrated life of phenomenal pursuits through the endless cycle of transmigration. Their spiritual ignorance compels them to live at the plane of sensory experiences and behave like the insects who fly voluntarily into the burning flame in the hope of permanently enjoying the company of its light.

Kabīra points out the futility of mere conceptual understanding and verbal repetition of the words of the revealed texts and the realized saints.[142] He exhorts the spiritually aspiring people to stop wasting time in verbal repetition of the revealed words. He asks them to instead look for the inner realization indicated by those revealed texts. It is utterly futile to comprehensively grasp the nature of the origin, sustenance and destruction of the phenomenal realm within the framework of language, logic and duality-based concepts. It is so because of the transcendent nature of the highest reality. That is, one cannot ever be successful in accommodating the transcendent reality within that which it transcends. However, since that transcendent reality is the ontological ground of the phenomenal realm, therefore the intuitive realization of its nature immediately reveals all the aspects of the phenomenal realm as well. The various accounts of supernatural powers exhibited by the realized saints at some points of time provide an indirect testimony to this fact.

Kabīra refers to the twin-fold spiritual disciplines practised even by the earliest Vedic sages such as Sanaka and Sanandana.[143] This ancient spiritual discipline aims at the intuitive realization of immutable *(akṣara)* Brahman. Its twin disciplines pertain to the intuitive realization of the immanent presence of the subtle light and vibration of the non-dual and absolute supreme Brahman. It aims at realizing the basic identity of the Self with that transcendent reality. However, despite the universal immanence of this subtle light and vibration, the worldly people do not witness them. Their senses only cognize the grosser manifestations of that light and vibration. But, by concentrating the mind and ridding it of all thoughts pertaining to the phenomenal realm, one can intuitively witness the light and vibration of the absolute non-dual consciousness, which is the same as one's Self and the supreme Brahman. Kabīra advocates the practice of this spiritual discipline, coupled with the practice of renunciation and discrimination, for attaining the liberative realization.

Kabīra further highlights the supreme importance of controlling one's mind.[144] He says that the spiritually aspiring people go on wandering in all the ten directions in search of the supreme reality but their unstable and scattered state of the mind prevents them from realizing its immanent presence in their own Self. If one somehow becomes successful in perfectly concentrating the mind even once, then the transcendent nature of the Self can certainly be realized. In the absence of such realization the worldly people, being unaware of their blissful non-dual Self, remain busy in the pursuit of the objects and gods of the dualistic realm.

Kabīra points out the great importance of a realized spiritual preceptor in the journey of spiritual realization.[145] He says that one is led astray by the phenomenal realm of duality only as long as one does not take refuge in the benevolent guidance of a realized preceptor. The dualities of the phenomenal realm reveal their illusory character by following the directions of the spiritual preceptor. However, rare are the souls who truly take refuge in the words of the realized preceptor. Such realized saints have been in the world in all ages and they have also been trying to show the correct spiritual path to the masses but despite all this, the vast majority of the worldly people do not pay any sincere attention to them. It is so because one does not even feel the need of spiritual realization and liberation unless and until one has earned a lot of karmic merit. Such people are always few in number. Only they are truly in search of the realized preceptors and the intuitive realization of the supreme reality. The perfectly realized saints always live in identity with the supreme Brahman and therefore the sermons of such saints are nothing short of clarion calls of the supreme Brahman itself. Yet, the unfortunate fact is that the worldly people are so engrossed with their material engagements that they go on foolishly overlooking the miserable nature of the phenomenal realm and thus they do not listen to the saving words of the realized saints.

Kabīra discusses the nature of the supreme reality and its intuitive realization.[146] He says that it is utterly impossible to describe the nature and form of the supreme Brahman in terms of phenomenal language and concepts. The reason of such inexpressibility is that it is non-dual in nature, whereas the phenomenal language and concepts can be significant only in a dualistic framework. He says further that nobody can ever possibly behold that supreme reality in the framework of subject-object duality. Therefore, in the moment of the supreme intuitive realization there remains nobody as a cognizer of that supreme reality. There is simply a revelation of the absolute and immutable nature of the non-dual Brahman as the universal Self. Therefore, even in the post-realization stage there can be no possibility of a positive description of the supreme reality in terms of phenomenal language and concepts.

Kabīra briefly describes the process of mind-control.[147] By sincerely practising sense-control, renunciation and concentration of the mind over the supreme Brahman, the mind ultimately becomes devoid of all dualistic thoughts. Then in that void of consciousness, Kabīra says, there occurs the revelation of the subtle light of the infinite and blissful consciousness of Brahman. Kabīra says that light is verily the non-dual supreme Brahman, the sole transcendent and yet universally immanent ontological reality. That supreme Brahman is the sole ontological ground of all that is there and all that can ever be. It is the support of all and it is not in need of any support itself.

Indicating the transcendent nature of the supreme Brahman, Kabīra says that before there was any epistemic projection of duality by the cosmic projective principle, namely *Māyā,* there was no trace of any phenomenal knowledge, not even of the so called eternal Vedas.[148] There were no gross vibrations or any kind of sense experiences. There were no microcosmic points of consciousness or even the physical bodies that could possibly inhabit them. At that point, there were neither the celestial regions, the nether regions, nor even the ordinary phenomenal regions. There was neither the space nor the sky and not even the other three basic elements. That is to say, the transcendent reality has no place for any of the basic objective principles of the phenomenal realm of duality. There is also no room for any sense of subjective individuality in that sphere. It is the purely transcendent sphere of non-duality.

Kabīra further says that it is impossible to talk of the deliberations of that immutable non-dual Brahman.[149] It lies beyond the range of space and time, since they are themselves the effects of epistemic projections brought about by the inalienable power of the supreme Brahman. Moreover, that non-dual Brahman is bereft of all identifiable phenomenal qualities and characteristics. That is why it is also referred to as the *Nirguṇa Nirākāra Brahman*. In such a scenario, how can there be the possibility of any positive description of that in terms of words and concepts. All phenomenal words and concepts implicitly presuppose the framework of space, time, causality, qualities, change, dualistic cognizability, etc. but none of these factors are available in the case of the supreme non-dual Brahman. As such, it is quite natural that it can never become an object of linguistic descriptions. It cannot be named positively. That is why the Upaniṣads refer to it negatively as *'neti-neti'*.

Kabīra reminds us that even the Upaniṣad *mahāvākyas* e.g., *'tattvamasi'* or 'That thou art' indicate the non-dual absoluteness of the supreme Brahman.[150] He says these statements are the highest conclusions of the Vedic Upaniṣads. They categorically point out the fundamental ontological identity of the Self and the supreme Brahman. In spite of all the contrary evidences witnessed in the phenomenal realm of duality, it is the absolute and non-dual nature of the Self and the highest reality that is the conclusion of the revealed knowledge of the Vedas. This greatest spiritual truth can be authoritatively taught by only those who have gained an intuitive insight into the non-dual nature of the Self and Brahman. Moreover, this profound spiritual truth cannot be given to one and all. The person must be having the strongest desire for the highest spiritual knowledge and liberation. He must also be possessing all the other necessary moral and spiritual merits. Only the truly eligible spiritual aspirants are capable of handling this most sublime spiritual truth. Only they can properly strive to realize it intuitively after receiving it from the realized spiritual preceptor.

Kabīra goes on to discuss the nature of authority associated with intuitive spiritual realizations.[151] He says that the realization of the supreme reality is not in need of any other verification or validation. It is its own indisputable authority. Being the pure non-dual consciousness, it is itself the ultimate validating ground of all the phenomenal pieces of knowledge. Its realization is self-verifying in the absolute sense of the term. The supreme reality is the infinite and immutable non-dual bliss and consciousness. Its realization reveals its nature in the most intimate manner possible i.e., in the manner of non-dual identity. It is the supreme *rasa,* the embodiment of infinite bliss. The experience of that bliss does not require anything else to verify it. Kabīra refers to the tradition of the great ancient sages such as Sanaka, Nārada, Śuka, Yājñavalkya, Janaka, etc. who had experienced that supreme bliss and declared that it is highest source and authority of all possible knowledge.

Kabīra indicates the process and completion of the spiritual journey of persons seeking the highest knowledge and liberation.[152] He says that even though the fetters of *Māyā* are so strong that even the gods cannot escape it, it is a fact that the regular practice of spiritual disciplines in the guidance of a realized preceptor has the power of breaking those bonds. The spiritual aspirant moves ahead in the path of spiritual realization by diligently practising the disciplines prescribed to him by his preceptor. The final destination of the spiritual journey arrives when he is able to stabilize his mind in the fourth sphere of consciousness called the *turīya avasthā*. Kabīra says that just as it befits a king to ride a grand horse, similarly spiritual adepts stabilize themselves in the fourth state of consciousness i.e., the transcendent sphere of non-dual Brahman.

Kabīra points out the supreme importance of practising spiritual disciplines in the right spirit.[153] He says that a devotee or spiritual aspirant surely comes to achieve that for which he strives, if he perseveres in the practice of his spiritual disciplines. This surety is the key to the highest realization as well as the source of numerous distractions in the path of realization. The devotees practising spiritual disciplines with the objective of attaining some phenomenal results, whether gross or subtle, come to achieve that only. The devotees desirous of dualistic results get that only; they do not seek and hence do not get the non-dual realization and its attendant liberation. The highest realization is possible only for those who do not have any desires pertaining to the realm of duality. It requires the highest renunciation, which is possible only through the constant practice of discrimination and sense-control. All this becomes possible only with the help of the realized preceptors. That is, only those who strive exclusively for the non-dual realization come to attain it by the grace of God and their preceptors.

Kabīra explains the need and method to realize the transcendent supreme Brahman as identical with one's Self.[154] He says that even though the phenomenal world seems to be full of various pleasures, the fact is that all the people suffer from innumerable miseries. The world is replete with hollow promises of phenomenal pleasures. One should be reflective and realize the ultimately miserable nature of worldly pleasures. The way to attain real and lasting bliss lies in the intuitive realization of the Self alone. That is why Kabīra exhorts one and all to sincerely practise the various spiritual disciplines in the guidance of some realized preceptor. The way to achieve the highest spiritual realization is somewhat on the lines of the *bhṛṁgī-kīṭa nyāya* according to which an ordinary insect takes on the form of a *bhṛṁgī* due to its absolute absorption in the idea of the *bhṛṁgī*. That is to say, when the mind of the spiritual aspirant completely banishes all dualistic ideas and gets totally absorbed in the nature of pure and non-dual consciousness, that consciousness reveals its innate identity with the transcendent non-dual Brahman.

Kabīra beautifully presents the universal immanence of the transcendent non-dual reality.[155] He says that those who understand that it is the same transcendent reality which has epistemically taken the form of the principal deities as well as the various individual souls have truly achieved the highest spiritual realization. It is imperative to realize intuitively three important aspects of reality and the Self. Firstly, one needs to realize the non-dual transcendent nature of the Self. Secondly, one needs to realize the identity of the Self with the transcendent supreme Brahman. Thirdly, one must also realize the universal immanence of the transcendent Brahman in the realm of phenomenal plurality, as also the fact that the cosmic projective principle is but the inalienable power of the supreme Brahman. Kabīra says that a person having an intuitive realization of such a nature disappoints both *Yama,* the god of death, and *Māyā,* the cosmic projective principle. That is to say, such a person completely breaks free from the primal ignorance and its resultant phenomenal bondage. He becomes a *jīvanmukta* as soon as he attains that sort of inner realization.

Kabīra wonders how can anyone sing the glories of that which is referred to as the 'unnameable'.[156] The supreme Brahman and the Self transcend the realm of duality and therefore it is not possible to describe them in terms of phenomenal language. However, there can be no doubt that the supreme reality is certainly capable of being intuitively realized in an indisputable manner. Kabīra compares people of such realization with the traveler sitting calmly in a river-boat. Just as the traveler does not seem to be doing anything and yet he is moving towards its destination continuously, similarly the realized person i.e., the *jīvanmukta,* does not appear to be exerting either for the phenomenal or the spiritual goals and yet he is surely progressing towards an absolute stabilization in the supreme Brahman in correspondence with the progressive fructification of his *prārabdha karmas*. The liberated-while-alive person does not have the usual pre-realizational sense of identity with the physical body. He has an innate calmness of the mind. He does not indulge in selfishly motivated worldly actions and he also does not gossip uselessly. Kabīra points out that in contrast to the worldly people, who always have a distracted state of mind, the *jīvanmukta* person never loses sight of the supreme reality even for a moment while living amidst all the dualistic experiences of the phenomenal realm.

Kabīra openly promises to one and all that if anyone takes refuge in him and follows his directions in a sincere manner, then in six months that person can have the intuitive realization of the supreme reality.[157] Kabīra says how can he show the content of his realization to the undeserving people since even if he wished to do it, it would not be possible. The worldly people do not have a developed intuitive faculty, which is necessary for appreciating and achieving any spiritual truth. The supreme spiritual realization is a hidden secret which is not noticeable from outside but which nonetheless transforms the entire personality of the realized person by making him aware of the basic identity of the Self and the supreme non-dual Brahman. Kabīra also laments over the fact that the worldly people are not interested in saving themselves and therefore he finds himself quite helpless in helping them spiritually. Nobody can save a person who is not interested in saving himself.

Kabīra tries to persuade the worldly people to listen to him by telling them the benefits of spiritual realization.[158] He addresses them as 'sons' as those who listen to him would be inheriting his spiritual wealth and wisdom. He cajoles them to accept his services in the form of spiritual guidance so that he may succeed in making the kingdom of spirit available to them, which truly belongs to them. He says that if they listen to him and follow his instructions then he would extricate them from the invincible fort of phenomenal ignorance and attachments. He promises them to show the entire process of the genesis and dissolution of the phenomenal realm. Those who attain the highest spiritual realization also come to intuitively witness the entire epistemic process of evolution and involution of the phenomenal realm out of the transcendent non-dual consciousness. Kabīra promises that having attained the supreme realization they would be enjoying the supreme and eternal bliss of Brahman within their very Self. All the possible pleasures of the phenomenal realm are but a trifle as compared with the bliss of Brahman. Having once tasted the bliss of Brahman, one cannot have any desire left for phenomenal enjoyments since they are all so insignificant in comparison with the intuitive bliss of self-realization. Kabīra promises that by winning the highest realization they would be safe against all kinds of harm. They would not have to face the phenomenal cycle of transmigration anymore. With the destruction of their primary ignorance, all their karmic seeds also lose their binding potency, except the case of already fructifying *prārabdha karmas*. He says they would realize infinite spiritual bliss. He asks them to take his promises as absolutely true. Kabīra says that only those who listen to him and follow his instructions can become the true saints. The idea is that only by listening to the words of realized preceptors one can hope to move ahead in the path of spiritual realization and ultimately attain the supreme realization of the identity of the non-dual Brahman and the Self. They alone can be privy to the epistemic process of evolution and involution ranging between the non-dual consciousness and the gross material world of duality.

Kabīra describes the bewildering cosmic play of the supreme reality in association with its inseparable projective power.[159] He says that the supreme Brahman alone is the ultimate ontological reality and it is non-dual and immutable as well. However, its inseparable projective power, *Māyā,* epistemically projects the illusion of duality and change, along with all the basic parameters of the phenomenal realm e.g., space, time, causality, etc. All the phenomenal manifestations of individuality, including that of the *jīvas,* are based in epistemic projections only. The underlying ontological reality of the entire phenomenal realm is that it does not have any reality apart from its basic identity with the supreme non-dual Brahman. The wonderous fact is that this play of duality and non-duality is all within Brahman only. As the transcendent non-dual ontological ground of everything, Brahman is pure and infinite bliss and consciousness. As the principle responsible for the cosmic epistemic projections, it is the magician exhibiting the cosmic dream of duality. As the reality manifesting itself in the forms of various phenomenal subjects and objects, it alone is also the spectator of this cosmic magic show. The fact is that the transcendent non-dual Brahman alone epistemically manifests in the form of one and all. Brahman alone is the transcendent yet universally immanent reality.

Kabīra says he loves only the true well-wishers of the spiritually ignorant people.[160] They are the ones dutifully engaged in bringing back the ignorant worldly people back to the path of true spiritual realization. Further, Kabīra says, the truly wise ones are those who are always in search of the right spiritual path until they come across some realized preceptor who helps them out of the worldly quagmire. Having once identified the proper spiritual path, they are never led astray from it. Kabīra says it is the highest duty of the spiritual preceptor to firmly set the disciple on the path of spiritual realization. A preceptor who fails in doing so is but a false preceptor. The true preceptor has to spiritually awaken the worldly people lost in the pride of their wealth and progeny so that they may personally realize the supreme reality in an intuitive manner.

Kabīra says that the worldly people have virtually become orphans due to their ignorance of the Self and Brahman.[161]

They are totally lost in the forest of worldly desires and they cannot find the way out of it. Their only hope lies in finding the loving guidance of some realized preceptor since no language and concept-based description of the highest reality is capable of presenting its true nature. The realized saints know that even the revealed texts, such as the Vedas, can at best present mere secondary and partial versions of the nature of that supreme reality. The realized preceptors know well that any amount of intellectual discussion is inherently incapable of revealing the true nature of the Self and the supreme Brahman. The knowers of the highest spiritual truth look at the phenomenal realm as a magical show presented by the projective power of the supreme Brahman, within that Brahman only. Kabīra says that God appreciates those people who live in the world even while being fully aware of its illusory nature. Persons having realization of the supreme non-dual Brahman also understand its universal immanence and thus witness its presence in each and every particle of the phenomenal realm. Their vision of the non-dual Brahman is unperturbed and undivided by the pluralistic facade of the phenomenal realm. Their steady state of the mind remains unruffled by the pleasant and painful experiences of the phenomenal realm, brought about by their *prārabdha karmas*. Kabīra says that the realized preceptors very well know who is ripe to receive the spiritual directions of the preceptor and if once the eligible spiritual aspirant comes to receive directions from a realized preceptor, then he certainly moves ahead to attain the highest spiritual realization, tasting which there can be no possibility of falling back into the morass of worldly life.

Discussing the nature, desirability and limitations of speech, Kabīra says that the nature of supreme reality cannot be conveyed through verbal discussions.[162] Language is inherently incapable of expressing the nature of any transcendent reality, as it transcends its range of validity. The moment anyone tries to linguistically describe the nature of the supreme reality, he inevitably ends up distorting its presentation. Kabīra advises that one should not talk of worldly matters too much since it only leads to enhancement of worldly attachments and aversions. One must first reflect over the worthiness of the topic of conversation. Kabīra says it is certainly desirable to have a short conversation with saintly persons but it always better to be silent on coming across mean-minded persons. It is always beneficial to talk to the wise and spiritual persons but by conversing with fools one can only become mentally disturbed. Kabīra says that those who know little are like half-filled vessels which make a lot of noise, but the truly knowledgeable persons speak less and that too after due reflection on its desirability.

Commenting on untouchability, Kabīra says that it is one of the worst facets of conventional religion and it constitutes a strong fetter of phenomenal bondage since it fosters a false sense of identity.[163] The false sense of superiority and inferiority resulting from the notions of one's caste is a huge impediment in the path of spiritual progress. One who comes to believe in the equality of all human beings due to their similar spiritual nature can no longer accept the notions of untouchability. For them, the real untouchables are the spiritually ignorant worldly people. The realized preceptors see the same supreme reality immanent in all the sentient and insentient phenomena. They transcend the worldly notions of morality and immorality, purity and impurity.

Kabīra clarifies the real meaning of the word 'Rāma'.[164] He says unequivocally that the Rāma he talks about is not the one who was born as the son of king Daśaratha and had later killed Rāvaṇa. He implores everybody not to forget that the real Rāma is the universally immanent reality only and that reality is just the same as the transcendent non-dual Brahman. Kabīra declares that the supreme reality does not have either a gross or a subtle form. All names and forms pertain to the realm of epistemically projected illusions only. The supreme reality is non-dual and formless. One must strive to intuitively realize that supreme reality since that is the only way of fully eradicating the various phenomenal miseries.

Kabīra says that even though the fetters of *Māyā* are very strong, the wise persons take refuge in the practice of spiritual disciplines for the purpose of attaining the highest spiritual realization.[165] He compares the practice of spiritual disciplines for the sake of realization, to a boat which can safely ferry the aspirant across the vast ocean of phenomenal miseries. Kabīra says that even though achieving the supreme realization is an extremely difficult task, one should not waver from the goal of such realization. If necessary, one must have the perseverance to go on moving in its direction through numerous phenomenal lives as well. But, one should not in any case lose heart and revert to the worldly life-style.

Kabīra points out the phenomenally incomprehensible nature of the supreme reality.[166] He says that there is only one absolute ontological reality and the entire phenomenal realm is but its epistemic manifestation. The bliss of that supreme reality alone manifests in a distorted and partial manner in all the phenomenal experiences of pleasure. The worldly people unknowingly look for the bliss of that reality only as manifesting partially in the phenomenal sphere, but the spiritually aware people strive to attain its infinite non-dual bliss through their intuitive realization. That supreme reality is immanent in all the subjects and objects of the phenomenal realm. No one can say whether it is a male or a female, whether it is light or heavy. It is totally beyond the realm of hunger and thirst, light and shade, pleasure and pain. Its form is infinite and the way to know it is the path of intuitive realization alone. However, any amount of meditative practice is incapable of providing a complete knowledge of that reality due to its infinite nature.

Kabīra brings out the crucial role of one's willingness to move ahead in the path of spiritual realization.[167] Complete dedication to the life of spiritual disciplines is required to attain the highest realization. If one is ever diligent in the path of spiritual disciplines, he goes on progressing, but if the person becomes complacent, his spiritual qualities are bound to get depleted. Spiritual progress and decay are directly commensurate with one's honesty and sincerity in the spiritual life. Kabīra says that the spiritual status and realization of a person is best known to that person himself. It is not a matter of external exhibition and even if one desires to show it to others, the task cannot be satisfactorily accomplished. The nature of spiritual realization is essentially internal and any effort to display it externally is but a misdirected effort. Kabīra wonders for how long he should go on talking about the realizational nature of true spirituality before the worldly people to motivate them for having their own realization. Kabīra says that if anyone cares for his words then he is most willing to give them more profound spiritual truths. He thus tries to show that in this world even though the realized saints are always there and willing to help, there is a great paucity of spiritually desirous eligible persons. It is so because only after leading a very reflective moral life through many births one becomes aware of the worthlessness of worldly life, which is a pre-requisite for the sincere search of spiritual realization.

Kabīra points out the paramount importance of discrimination.[168] He says that any amount of zealous effort becomes useless in the spiritual realm if it is not supported by discrimination between the right and wrong in the spiritual sense. It is difficult to see the face of reality even in one's dreams without the constant practice of discrimination *(viveka)*. He compares the lot of the undiscriminating person to that of a foolish trader who cannot distinguish between good and bad items and thus ends up losing even his capital while trying to make profit. Spiritual discrimination can be learnt only from the adepts in that field i.e., the realized saints. It primarily constitutes in understanding the difference between the ephemeral duality-based objects and experiences and the transcendent and immutable non-dual consciousness and bliss of supreme Brahman. Its purpose is to free the mind from the phenomenal thoughts and thus facilitate its concentration on the transcendent Self and Brahman.

Kabīra describes the nature of the true *kṣatriya*.[169] He says that the real *kṣatriya* is the person who fights with his unruly mind and senses. He subdues the mind and the five sense-organs with the constant practice of discrimination and renunciation and being successful in that he comes to realize the true nature of the Self. Kabīra says that the worldly *kṣatriya-s* who are always engaged in amassing wealth by the use of force are a pitiable lot since their life is wasted in no time at all. Instead of wasting one's courage and energy for the sake of phenomenal goods, the wise ones should make good use of it in the spiritual field. The effort and courage required in controlling the mind and senses is much greater as compared to what is necessary in the phenomenal realm.

Kabīra implores everybody not to be asleep spiritually while being physically awake.[170] He says that while the true nature of the self is beyond all phenomenal changes and mortality, the worldly people go on imagining themselves as being qualified by all sorts of phenomenal limitations. The state of a worldly person is truly amazing since the mind and the senses hold a total sway over the consciousness itself, whereas the fact is that consciousness alone provides the cognitive capacity to the mind and the senses. The mind of the worldly person calls the shots even though it is not primarily conscious. Kabīra compares this with a situation where a hare is seen to devour a lion. Kabīra further says that just as water does not fill up an inverted pitcher but it fills it up quickly when immersed in the right position, similarly when a realized preceptor is approached in the right spirit then the spiritual aspirant is quickly released from his ignorance and bondage. The spiritually awakened person is not interested in the external phenomenal objects. Rather, he witnesses the entire phenomenal realm emerging from the non-dual consciousness of the Self in his intuitive realizations. The perfect concentration of the mind on consciousness itself reveals the true nature of the Self. Such people are not so much interested in the phenomenal conversations. They are instead continuously immersed in the subtle inner vibration of the *anāhata śabda*. Kabīra says that the story of spiritual realization is quite wonderous. The spiritual adepts reverse the epistemic evolutionary sequence of the various elements. That is, they witness the internal epistemic dissolution of the earth element into the water element, then the water into the fire, the fire into the air, the air into the ether and lastly the ether element into the mind element. Finally, the mind element is merged back into the non-dual consciousness that is identical with the supreme Brahman. While coming out of the state of *samādhi,* the various basic principles are epistemically projected out of the non-dual consciousness in the reverse sequence. The realized persons imbibe the bliss of immortality in their intuitive realizational states. Kabīra says that those who succeed in tasting the infinite bliss of the supreme Brahman escape from the cycle of births and deaths. Having realized their identity with the transcendent Brahman, they enjoy its infinite and immutable bliss forever.

Kabīra points out the dilemma involved in trying to convey the nature of the supreme reality, as realized in the highest meditative state.[171] He says nobody would believe him if he said the truth to the worldly people. But, the fact is that it is a matter of verifiable intuitive experience. He says there is no customer of the invaluable uncut diamond of the form of knowledge of the supreme Brahman. But, the knowers of the supreme Brahman witness its subtle light in each and every corner of the universe. Kabīra says that even though the supreme reality is bereft of all qualities and it is not cognizable in the dualistic framework, one can realize it by the grace of the spiritual preceptor. One realizes the Self as one with the supreme Brahman in the *sahaja unmani samādhi*. Kabīra says once a person realizes that supreme reality, the mind remains forever immersed in its universal immanence and immutable transcendence. Kabīra says that he is preaching only what he has received from his own preceptor.

Kabīra points out the omnipotence and absolute freedom of God, the phenomenal manifestation of the supreme Brahman.[172] He says that if it is the wish of God, a beggar can become a king and a king can become a beggar in no time. He has made the clove trees which do not bear any fruit, whereas the sandal tree does not bear any fruit or flower. He has made the vast ocean of phenomenal existence wherein the great prey-fish, *Māyā,* holds sway over all the beings and the self, though being all powerful like a lion, is seemingly lost. He says that the realization of the supreme reality transforms the spiritual aspirant into a venerable saint, whose love and knowledge purifies the ten directions. Kabīra says that by the grace of God even the blinds can witness the entire phenomenal universe in their intuitive visions. His grace can enable the lame cross the mountains and the mute spread the light of knowledge with the help of the *anāhata śabda*. Kabīra says God can change the order of the skies and the earth if He so wishes. The crux of the matter is that God is the supreme master of the universe and whatever He does will only suit Him.

Kabīra indicates the paucity of the spiritually realized and interested people in this world.[173] He says he has very few friends. He says it is God alone who makes and mars everything in the world. Therefore, the spiritually awake persons remain content with whatever God provides them with. Kabīra says that it is very rare for the pundits indulging in vast scriptural studies to realize the supreme reality, since they seldom know how to control their minds and senses. He says it is futile to pin one's spiritual hopes on persons making a pompous show of their spiritual status. They are mere traders in the name of spirituality. On the other hand, those who persevere in their spiritual disciplines with true devotion to God certainly attain the highest spiritual realization by the grace of God in due course of time.

Kabīra clearly puts across the point that the realized persons look beyond the various distinctions based in phenomenal conventions, even when they are sought to be propagated in the name of religion and spirituality.[174] He wonders how it became possible for the people of different religious communities to think that their God was different from those of the other communities. He wonders who could have misled whom. The so-called different gods have been given different names but this should not mislead one to think that they are really different from one another. Kabīra takes the example of gold and various gold ornaments. He says that all the gold ornaments are made of gold only and in that sense, they are not substantially different from one another. It is only the names and forms of the different gold ornaments that is suggestive of their separate identities, but such a suggestion is quite misleading. It is only on account of one's distance from God that one fails to grasp the true nature of God. It is such spiritual ignorance only that nourishes the idea of the separate identities of the gods of different communities. Kabīra further says that even the modes of worshipping God are given different names in different communities, but this should not mislead one to think of their substantially different ways of approaching God. Actually, they all are just different names for devotionally approaching God in the different communities. It is a difference of name only. He says both the Hindus and the Muslims live on the same earth created by God. Their scriptures have different names but, being revealed texts, they all talk of the same reality. Their priestly classes have different names but they perform the same tasks. Kabīra says that they all are different pots fashioned out of the same clay and thus they have been assigned different names. But, their different names should not lead us to think that their substantial nature is basically different as well. Kabīra says that those who are stuck at the conventional levels of their religious identities are spiritually ignorant people. They do not realize the all-encompassing nature of the supreme reality. They waste their lives in useless discussions and fights. Kabīra, therefore, pleads before them to look at the common reality underlying the web of communal and conventional distinctions. One needs to develop the spiritual insight to appreciate the absolute nature of the supreme reality.

Kabīra talks of the effect of the company of spiritually enlightened persons.[175] He humorously warns the worldly people not to live in the vicinity of the spiritual practitioners because there is the danger of getting attracted towards the life of spirituality. They preach things that are the antithesis of the worldly lifestyle. But, Kabīra says, despite all these oddities, it is a fact that such people have access to the great medicine of immortality. Those who successfully understand the secret of the spiritual adepts, find themselves merged in the supreme non-dual reality. They witness the universal immanence of that supreme reality. Imbibing the bliss of the transcendent Brahman, such people escape the cycle of phenomenal transmigrations.

Kabīra declares that he has now seen through the magical show of the supreme reality that is being projected by its bewildering *Māyā*.[176] He says that the cosmic magical show of duality goes on for some duration after which it is all withdrawn back into the basic ontological reality, namely the non-dual supreme Brahman. The magical show of God is so perplexing that even great sages and celestial beings are easily misled by it. They lose their hold on spiritual knowledge. But, the spiritually realized persons know with absolute certainty that it is only the magician that is real and not the projected magical show of phenomenal duality. Kabīra says that it is in accordance with one's understanding of reality that one has to go through various experiences. Those who take the world of duality as real, remain in it to go through its various good and bad experiences, whereas those who take the non-dual transcendent reality alone as real, see through the illusion of duality and as a result of it they are freed from the cycle of transmigrations.

Thus, it has been seen that the concept of knowledge and liberation is multi-faceted in eyes of Kabīra. He clearly takes liberation to be a direct implication of the highest possible spiritual knowledge. He clearly distinguishes between theoretical knowledge and realizational knowledge. According to him, it is not possible to move ahead in the spiritual path without the help and guidance of a realized preceptor. One has to continuously practise renunciation and discrimination, along with the control of sense organs to progress towards the highest spiritual realization. The highest spiritual knowledge reveals both the transcendent and immanent aspects of the supreme reality. It also makes known the epistemic process of the projection of the dualistic universe out of the non-dual and immutable supreme Brahman. A realized saint thus comes to know the supreme reality in both its ontological and epistemic aspects. He lives in phenomenal realm as a *jīvanmukta* as long as his *prārabdha karmas* are still fructifying, after which he attains the irreversible liberation of absolute identity with the non-dual transcendent Brahman.

Chapter V

The Towering Uniqueness of Kabīra

Kabīra had a multi-faceted personality. He was a philosopher, saint and social-religious reformer of the highest order. His whole life was an illustrious example of love, mercy, knowledge, honesty, truthfulness, spiritual realization, renunciation and discrimination. The different aspects of his personality were mutually dependent and interactive. As such, it is logical to treat these various aspects in a holistic manner. Its deliberate segmentation can only be at the cost of its comprehensive understanding. Yet, the most that one can possibly do is to try and identify the most fundamental aspect of his personality.

It is very clear that Kabīra gave the highest importance to the spiritual life of a person. For him, the highest aim and obligation of human life is to attain the intuitive realization of the supreme non-dual Brahman.[177] But the mute question is why should one look for that liberative realization at all? The answer to this question reveals the philosophical thoughts of Kabīra. The completion of Kabīra's philosophical task sets the stage for his spiritual development and realization. Lastly, the completion of his spiritual task paves the way for the reformist stage of his life.

Thus, one can see the development of the various stages of his personality in a sequential and logical order. However, out of these three aspects of his personality, it is not difficult to grasp the centrality of the spiritual aspect.[178] The problems and the agenda set forth by the philosophical stage of his development find their answers in the succeeding spiritual stage, whereas the realizational conclusions discovered in the spiritual stage serve as the foundation of the succeeding reformist stage of his development. The pivotal role of spirituality in the life of Kabīra is therefore beyond all doubts. For Kabīra, the touchstone of spirituality is the ultimate criterion for the acceptance or rejection of any idea, practice or value.

Thus, it would be logical to see the development of Kabīra's personality through the stages of philosopher, saint and lastly reformer. However, in the very process of such development, Kabīra had exhibited his uniqueness in many respects. An inquiry into the special status of Kabīra requires one to locate his points of uniqueness in all the three developmental stages of his life and personality.

Let us first of all take up the developmental stage of the philosopher Kabīra. Like all philosophers Kabīra too was concerned about the nature, problems and goals of human existence, apart from the general nature of reality. He had also paid proper attention to the nature of human knowledge. Kabīra gave great importance to common sense and refused to be swept away by intricate speculative argumentations if they turned out to be in conflict with one's common sense. He did not accept speculative philosophy as a proper way of understanding the nature of reality.[179] He was very clear on the point that mere verbal arguments and expositions do not prove anything and they do not benefit anyone.

He was awestruck by the universality of the nature of worldly people and their manner of deliberations. They all betrayed the same pattern of material hopes, pursuits and final frustrations at some point or the other. The twin reality of material aspirations and the inevitable exposure of the hollow promise of phenomenal bliss and security was well noticed by Kabīra.[180] He wondered as to why people do not learn from the mistakes of so many other people. Why is it that they go on entertaining those very phenomenal aspirations which are never fulfilled in the true sense of the term? What is the reason for their developing such aspirations in the first place? All these questions posed themselves before Kabīra on the basis of his common experience of the world and his common sense.

The usual philosophical answers to these questions could not satisfy Kabīra. The reason was the extremely speculative nature of those answers. Those answers did not satisfy either the common sense or the philosophical intellect. Ultimately speaking, they just presented the philosophical problems as a given fact of the phenomenal realm. The answers to those questions had to be speculative when attempted within the framework of phenomenal logic, language and rationality.

The philosopher Kabīra was thus convinced that the explanations and answers to the ironies and problems of phenomenal existence could not be found within the phenomenal realm itself.[181] They had to be sought somewhere else.

At this point Kabīra noticed another startling fact of the phenomenal realm. He saw that the saints of various traditions had a unique similarity in terms of their peace and satisfaction, despite leading a life of austerity and self-control.[182] This was a sort of direct contradiction to the aspirations and reality of the worldly people. The worldly people seek to achieve peace and happiness by amassing wealth and the various objects of sense enjoyment. They are always busy in this phenomenal pursuit, not knowing where to stop it. Moreover, there is no limit to this pursuit either.[183] Further, even those who are generally considered quite successful in their worldly exploits, do not claim to have attained the peace and satisfaction they were hoping to attain at the end of their pursuit. In fact, the usual refrain is that the pursuit is still going on and so the goal is not achieved as yet. A normal human life-span always proves extremely insufficient for the fulfillment of the phenomenal agenda.

In contrast, the saints are always so calm and loving that there can be no doubt about their having achieved that much wanted lasting peace and happiness. However, the worldly understanding of the way to such peace and happiness is not corroborated by the lives of saints. Kabīra was quick in noticing that the inevitable failure of the worldly people and the general success of the saintly people in achieving a lasting sense of peace and happiness indisputably pointed towards the validity of the spiritual framework of the saints. Kabīra's philosophical outlook, which was based in his common sense and ordinary observations of the world around him, thus took him to the threshold of the spiritual life.

Thus, the philosophical mind of Kabīra was never satisfied with doing philosophy for the sake of philosophy. For him, philosophy was meant to serve the purpose of human needs and aspirations. He compared the philosophers indulging in mere hair-splitting arguments to asses carrying loads of books or sandalwood who never draw any benefit from those things.[184] Kabīra's stance was that mere theoretical understanding and satisfaction cannot be sufficient; it is necessary for knowledge to percolate down to the level of existence and experience in the true sense of the term. A detailed and sophisticated discussion of the nature of knowledge would be of no use if it did not help us in moving towards that real knowledge. Similarly, a profound discussion of the nature of happiness would not carry any worth if it did not help us in moving towards a lasting happiness. Philosophy can be relevant only if it is based in common sense and designed to serve the purpose of human existence and aspirations, in the broad sense of the term. Kabīra's philosophy was not an elitist one. It was meant to serve the purpose of the common man by appealing to his common sense and general experience of the world. The philosophical engagement of Kabīra thus paved the way for his spiritual life.

Kabīra was a saint of the highest order and he had the highest intuitive realization. He was very emphatic about the need of a spiritual preceptor to guide one into the spiritual life.[185] The reason was very simple. The spiritual realm is the field of one's intuitive faculty and this faculty is not properly developed in the case of worldly people. To be initiated in this field requires a developed intuitive faculty. However, the worldly people do not have any firsthand knowledge of the nature of this faculty. They do not know how to develop it. Without the support of the intuitive faculty one can only be at the mercy of second-hand descriptions of reality given by the religious preachers. One would not be in a position to personally verify the truth of their expositions at all. Moreover, mere intellectual understanding of their discourses about the nature of the supreme reality cannot benefit the listener in the spiritual sense at all. Kabīra used to say that if by merely repeating the word 'sugar' one could have tasted it and got nourishment out of it, then spiritual realization and its resultant liberation would have been easily available for one and all.[186] But, such is never the case. Therefore, there is a categorical need for developing the intuitive faculty.

In order to achieve this objective, one needs to take the guidance and help of a realized preceptor since he has traversed the whole distance in the spiritual field. He knows the ins and outs of that field. Kabīra, therefore, highlighted the absolute importance of a realized preceptor in the field of spirituality. Any amount of studying even the revealed texts can never be a substitute for the realized preceptor.[187] He says a mirror is useless to a blind person. Kabīra also points out how a person can come across the right preceptor, even though it seems to be a matter of mere fate and coincidence. He says that when a person sincerely practices honesty, modesty and truthfulness, while praying to God to send him his spiritual preceptor, he definitely comes across his preceptor very soon.[188] God himself takes care of the spiritual needs of his devotees. On the other hand, even when a person comes across some realized preceptor, without having himself secured the requisite level of mental purity, either he would not appreciate the spiritual status of that saint or else even after repeated requests he would not be accepted as a disciple by that saint. Therefore, it is imperative to acquire the necessary eligibility for being accepted as a disciple by the qualified preceptor. Kabīra has repeatedly pointed out that there are very few worthy disciples in the world.

Although Kabīra gave great importance to the spiritual preceptor of a person and pointed out the necessity of following his directions in letter and spirit, he gave the highest importance to the knowledge derived from one's own intuitive realizations. This becomes clear from the fact that although Rāmānanda, the Guru of Kabīra, believed in Rāma as the incarnation of supreme reality, Kabīra never accepted the possibility of an incarnation of the supreme reality.[189] To him, Rāma simply meant the all-pervasive immanent and transcendent non-dual reality.[190] This spiritual conviction of Kabīra derived from his intuitive realizations and he stuck to it even at the cost of differing from his own preceptor.

Kabīra did not believe in the outward show of spirituality at all.[191] In fact, he believed that it ultimately harmed the spiritual life of a person by inflating his sense of ego. He always emphasized upon the purity of one's mind, heart and tongue. He used to say that God is not far away from the people who have achieved perfect correspondence between the heart and the tongue.[192] He presented truthfulness as the highest spiritual virtue. In fact, he mocked at people spending lot of time in maintaining external purity of the body, while being totally careless about the purity of mind and heart. External purity, without the purity of the mind, is spiritually worthless.[193] On the other hand, purity of the mind is always a spiritual excellence, whether it is accompanied by external purity or not.

Kabīra never advocated renouncing the world and taking refuge in the forests.[194] He only advocated the internal renunciation of attachment to the various phenomenal objects, since even in a forest one would have to be concerned about the maintenance of the physical body. In this context he also advised people to respect manual work and contribute towards the welfare of society by doing some useful work.[195] Despite the spiritual realization of the ultimate illusoriness of the phenomenal realm, he never advocated to neglect it altogether. A fine balance has to be achieved between the phenomenal and the spiritual lives, in which the spiritual one has to accorded the dominant position. Therefore, while living in the world one has to be very careful in seeing that one does not start accumulating phenomenal goods in a selfish manner.[196] One should not be developing attachment or aversion towards various phenomenal objects and experiences. The worldly life of a person should be only for discharging one's worldly duties, for the welfare of other people in society and the maintenance of one's physical body in a frugal manner.

Kabīra gave the highest importance to the meditative and realizational aspects of spirituality.[197] All the other aspects are important only to the extent of facilitating it. Purity of heart and a life of self-control, renunciation and discrimination are crucial for making spiritual progress. He did not believe in any complicated meditative procedure. According to him, the highest realization can be attained in an easy and natural manner. That is why he called the state of perfect meditative absorption *'sahaja samādhi'*.[198] One only needs to perfectly withdraw the mind from all thoughts about the phenomenal realm and focus it upon the nature of consciousness itself. The moment the mind becomes perfectly focused on consciousness itself, the revelation of the true nature of the Self takes place. It reveals itself as the infinitely blissful and immutable non-dual consciousness. Its pure nature is revealed to be transcendent to the realm of phenomenal duality. It reveals itself as the sole ontological absolute, identical with the supreme Brahman. Kabīra says that the highest intuitive realization reveals the Self as the immutable and transcendent non-dual supreme Brahman.

However, that is only one aspect of the highest realization. Its other equally important aspect is the realization that the entire phenomenal realm of duality is a mere epistemic projection out of the transcendent and immutable non-dual consciousness. Such epistemic projection takes place neither as a matter of desire or need. It occurs simply because of the projective nature of the inseparable power of the supreme Brahman, namely *Māyā*.[199]

This aspect of the intuitive realization leads Kabīra to witness the light and vibration of that supreme Brahman in each and every particle of the phenomenal universe. The spiritual outlook of Kabīra is quite unique because even though he maintains the ontological absoluteness and immutability of Brahman, he also accepts the spiritual worth of the phenomenal realm, despite knowing very well about the illusoriness of its names and forms. The reason is that he does not see only the names and forms constituting the phenomenal realm. He sees much more than that. He sees the indivisible ontological reality underlying the pluralistic phenomenal world.[200] He sees the inseparable power of the supreme Brahman being involved in the epistemic projection of the phenomenal realm. He looks at the phenomenal world as the realm of ignorance and bondage, as well as an opportunity for spiritually working the way out of it. If the world is full of objects of attachment and aversion, it is also the residence of great saints and the place of immense spiritual opportunities. It is up to the concerned person to be either foolish or discriminating. As one decides, so one acts and so one reaps the fruits in this world. Kabīra is unique in not being single-sided in his spiritual outlook.

Kabīra is also unique in maintaining the supreme status of the non-dual Brahman, along with the supreme controlling authority of *Īśvara,* the primary manifestation of the supreme Brahman in the realm of duality. Kabīra clearly accepts that ultimately it is *Īśvara* and *Māyā* who control the realm of duality.[201] He is absolutely clear about the ontological hierarchy of the supreme non-dual Brahman and its numerous dualistic manifestations. He does not deny the reality and authority of *Īśvara* to maintain the supreme status of the non-dual Brahman or vice-versa. He does not find any conflict between the two. Rather, he looks at them as two aspects of the same reality.[202]

Kabīra is also unique in his manner of behaviour towards the worldly people. He does not remain secretive about his spiritual realizations and conclusions. He also does not remain restricted in his teachings to his own disciples. He comes out openly and publicly before the worldly people in warning them of their ultimate worldly fate, exposing their greedy and hypocritical manners, in the effort to persuade them to make good use of the rare human life in moving towards spiritual realization.[203] He goes on doing it even to the displeasure of the worldly people. Sometimes, he does it even at the risk of his personal safety and security. Such commitment to spiritually bail out the worldly people, whether they like it or not, is certainly unique.

Although Kabīra gave great importance to being sweet and polite in speech and behaviour, he did not hesitate in rebuking and even abusing the hypocritical, greedy and cunning worldly people.[204] Even though such behaviour may seem rather unsaintly, the real reason behind such behaviour could have only been his unconditional love and concern for them and their spiritual welfare.

Kabīra's spiritual realization set him on a vast and dangerous reformist path. He took up the challenge of pointing out the follies of various influential sections in the fields of social institutions, religious practices, academic institutions, political institutions, etc. He never hesitated in fearlessly pointing out the unpalatable things coming to his notice. He relentlessly fought against the evil practice of untouchability and casteism.[205] He severely criticized indulgence in excessive accumulation and enjoyment of phenomenal objects.[206] He fought against the ritualism and sophistry of religious preachers of both the Hindus and the Muslims.[207] He criticized harshly the practice of killing animals either in the name of sacrifices or in the name of plane gluttony.[208] He criticized the incessant fights going on between different religious communities.

In all these various reformist activities, Kabīra maintained his uniqueness in a common measure. No matter whom he criticized, he never did it for the sake of promoting the interest of any one particular group of people at the cost of others. Whether it was the oppressed or the oppressor, he thought of the welfare of both. His reformist activities were not at the plane of phenomenal understanding. They were all grounded in his spiritual outlook to the world.

The uniqueness of Kabīra as a reformer lies in the fact that all his reformist activities were the direct implications of his sublime spiritual realizations. His arguments were based in his realizations. His concern for reforms was also ultimately spiritual in nature. He felt the need for reforms in various fields due to the conflict of the given state of affairs with the supreme nature of reality. This opposition also meant that the given state of affairs was quite obstructive to the spiritual development of the concerned people. Therefore, Kabīra used to feel the imperative need of frontally addressing the evil institutions and practices of his times. His effort was always to make the people see the problems and foolishness involved with such practices. He just wanted to wean away the people from the evil practices so that they may have the opportunity of developing spiritually.

The development of Kabīra's personality through the stages of a philosopher, a saint and a reformer, is focused around the highest objective of human beings *per se* viz. the attainment of peace and happiness in an infinite and immutable manner. His philosophical observations, analyses and conclusions were all with respect to the above mentioned ultimate human objective and aspiration. His life as a saint and his efforts for attaining the highest spiritual realization were nothing but an effort to realize that ultimate human objective. His supreme realization was the actualization of that ultimate aspiration in the form of realizing the basic identity of the Self with the transcendent, non-dual and infinitely blissful supreme Brahman. Having once achieved that perennial human dream, Kabīra could not restrain himself from going all out to help the intensely suffering worldly people. He could not care less whether to alleviate the suffering of the masses he had to persuade them or rebuke them or tempt them or even fight with the prevailing evil practices and their propagators. His sympathetic agony was so overpowering because he had realized in the most certain manner that what the world was searching for madly is already there with them and it had always been with them. He felt it as his spiritual obligation to do anything and everything to make the world realize it.

References

[1] *sakala kurāna kabīra hai, harapha likhe jo lekha; kāsī ke kājī kahaiṃ, gaī dīna kī ṭeka;* Kabīra Mansūr, p.253, (as quoted in Kabīra Darśana, p.24).

[2] Kabīra Caritrabodha, p.6, (as quoted in Kabīra Darśana, p.15).

[3] Ādi Guru Granth Sāhib (Taran-Tāran), p.698, (as quoted in Kabīra Darśana, p.10);
also,
Kabīra Darśana, p.11.

[4] Bhaktamāla, chappaya 31, (as quoted in Kabīra Darśana, p.7).

[5] *ati athāha jala gahara gaṃbhīra, bāṃdhi jaṃjīra jail bore haiṃ kabīra;*

jala kī taraṃga uṭhi kaṭihaiṃ jaṃjīra, hari sumirana taṭa baiṭhehaiṃ kabīra;

Kabīra Granthāvalī, p.203;

also,

bāṃdhi bhujā bhalaiṃ kari ḍāryo, hastī kopi muṇḍa maiṃ māryo;

bhāryo hastī cīsā mārī, vā mūrati kī maiṃ balihārī;

ibid., p.210.

[6] *bīsa saū laga kīnī bhagatī, tā pīchai pāī hai mukatī;*

(as quoted in Kabīra Darśana, p.46).

[7] *jau tana kāsī tajahi kabīrā rāmahi kahā nihorā,*

kahu kabīra sunahu re loī, bharama na bhūlahu koī,

kyā kāsī kyā ūsaru magahara rāma hiradaya jau hoī;

Kabīra Granthāvalī, p.291.

[8] *vai kahai gāroṃ vai kahai jārauṃ, apanī apanī dharama vicāroṃ;*

duhu ora tai deṣana āvai, sejahi phūla kabīra pāvai;

Paricayī Sāhitya, p.110, (as quoted in Kabīra Darśana, p.48).

[9] *je vo eka jāṃṇiyāṃ, tau jāṃṇyā saba jāṃṇa;*

je o eka jāṃṇiyāṃ, to sabahīṃ jāṃṇa ajāṃṇa;

Kabīra Granthāvalī, p.19.

[10] *sata gura tata kahyau bicāra, mūla gahyau anabhai bistāra;*

ibid., p.216.

[11] *aṃtara joti sabada eka nārī, hari brahmā tāke tripurārī;*

Bījaka., p.1.

[12] *brahmaṇḍe so pyaṇḍe jāṃni, māṃnasarovara kari asanāṃna;*

Kabīra Granthāvalī, p.199.

[13] ibid., p.216.

[14] *tetau āhi nināra niraṃjanāṃ, ādi anādi na āṃna;*

kahana sunana kauṃ kīnha jaga, āpai āpa bhulāṃna;

ibid., p.227.

[15] *āpahi bīja bṛccha aṅkurā āpa phūla phala chāyā;*

āpahi sūra kirina parakāsā āpa brahma jīva māyā;

Kabīra Vacanāvalī, p.203, (as quoted in Kabīra Darśana, p.175).

[16] *sāca soī je thiraha rahāī, upajai binasai jhūṭha hvai jāī;*

Kabīra Granthāvalī, p.233.

[17] Bījaka, Ramainī, 63.3, p.122.

[18] Kabīra Granthāvalī, p.20.

[19] ibid, pp.39f;

also,

Yoga-sūtra, 2-38.

[20] Bījaka, Ramainī, 1.1, p.1;

also,

Taittirīya Upaniṣad, 3-1;

also,

Brahma-sūtra, 1-1-1, p.13.

[21] Bījaka, Ramainī, 62, p.120.

[22] ibid, Ramainī, 30, p.230.

[23] ibid, Śabda, 4, pp.174f.

[24] ibid, Śabda, 70, p.313;

also,

Ādi Guru Granth Séhib (Taran-Tāran), p.698, (as quoted in Kabīra Darśana, p.10).

[25] Kabīra Granthāvalī, p.58.

[26] Bījaka, Ramainī, 1.1, p.1.

[27] ibid, Ramainī, 1.2, p.10.

[28] ibid, Ramainī, 1.9, p.16.

[29] ibid, Ramainī, 1.11, p.17.

[30] ibid, Ramainī, 1.13, p.18.

[31] ibid, Ramainī, 2.1, p.20.

[32] ibid, Ramainī, 2.2, p.24.

[33] ibid, Ramainī, 2.3, p.24.

[34] ibid, Ramainī, 2.4, 2.5, p.25.

[35] ibid, Ramainī, 2.6, p.26.

[36] ibid, Ramainī, 3.1, p.27.

[37] ibid, Ramainī, 3.2, p.28.

[38] ibid, Ramainī, 5.1, p.31.

[39] ibid, Ramainī, 5.2, p.31.

[40] ibid, Ramainī, 5.3, p.32.

[41] ibid, Ramainī, 5.5, p.32.

[42] ibid, Ramainī, 6.1, p.33.

[43] ibid, Ramainī, 6.4, p.35.

[44] ibid, Ramainī, 7.4, p.36.

[45] ibid, Ramainī, 8.1, p.37.

[46] ibid, Ramainī, 21.4, p.60.

[47] ibid, Ramainī, 26.5, p.67.

[48] ibid, Ramainī, 30.1, p.73.

[49] ibid, Ramainī, 37.3, p.84.

[50] ibid, Ramainī, 41.2, p.90.

[51] ibid, Ramainī, 42.1, p.92.

[52] ibid, Ramainī, 42.3, p.92.

[53] ibid, Ramainī, 63.3, p.122.

[54] ibid, Ramainī, 68.2, p.132.

[55] ibid, Ramainī, 77, pp.150-1.

[56] ibid, Śabda, 1, p.164.

[57] ibid, Śabda, 4.8, p.175.

[58] ibid, Śabda, 5, p.177.

[59] ibid, Śabda, 7.1, p.180.

[60] ibid, Śabda, 8.11, p.183.

[61] ibid, Śabda, 18.1, 18.5, p.204.

[62] ibid, Śabda, 22.1, p.211.

[63] ibid, Śabda, 27.1-2, p.222.

[64] ibid, Śabda, 43, p.250.

[65] ibid, Śabda, 75, p.323.

[66] ibid, Śabda, 78.3, p.327.

[67] ibid, Śabda, 83.1, p.336.

[68] ibid, Śabda, 94, pp.360-1.

[69] ibid, Śabda, 101.1-2, p.374.

[70] ibid, Śabda, 111.1, p.393.

[71] ibid, Śabda, 115.1,115.5, p.403.

[72] ibid, Jñāna Cauṁtīsā, 12, p.412.

[73] ibid, Jñāna Cauṁtīsā, 16, p.414.

[74] ibid, Jñāna Cauṁtīsā, 26, p.419.

[75] ibid, Vipramatīsī, 12, p.431.

[76] ibid, Vipramatīsī, 13, p.431.

[77] ibid, Kaharā, 1.1, p.433.

[78] ibid, Vasanta, 1.1, p.463.

[79] ibid, Vasanta, 1.4, p.463.

[80] ibid, Cācara, 1.1, p.491.

[81] ibid, Belī, 1.1-2, p.501.

[82] ibid, Birahulī, 1, p.510.

[83] ibid, Hiṃḍolā, 2.1, p.520.

[84] ibid, Sākhī, 4, p.528.

[85] ibid, Sākhī, 27, p.538.

[86] ibid, Sākhī, 35, p.543.

[87] ibid, Sākhī, 69, p.559.

[88] ibid, Sākhī, 272, p.654.

[89] ibid, Sākhī, 273, p.654.

[90] ibid, Sākhī, 347, p.690.

[91] ibid, Sākhī, 352, p.692.

[92] Bījaka, Ramainī, 1.6, p.12.

[93] ibid, Ramainī, 1.7, p.15.

[94] ibid, Ramainī, 1.9, p.16.

[95] ibid, Ramainī, 1.10, p.16.

[96] ibid, Ramainī, 1.13, p.18.

[97] ibid, Ramainī, 3.3, p.28.

[98] ibid, Ramainī, 4.1, p.29.

[99] ibid, Ramainī, 4.3, p.30.

[100] ibid, Ramainī, 5.1, p.31.

[101] ibid, Ramainī, 5.3, p.32.

[102] ibid, Ramainī, 5.4, p.32.

[103] ibid, Ramainī, 5.6, p.33.

[104] ibid, Ramainī, 7.2, p.36.

[105] ibid, Ramainī, 9.1, p.38.

[106] ibid, Ramainī, 9.2, p.39.

[107] ibid, Ramainī, 9.3, p.39.

[108] ibid, Ramainī, 9.4, p.40.

[109] ibid, Ramainī, 10.4, p.41.

[110] ibid, Ramainī, 12.4, p.44.

[111] ibid, Ramainī, 15.2, p.51.

[112] ibid, Ramainī, 18.2, p.56.

[113] ibid, Ramainī, 20.3, p.58.

[114] ibid, Ramainī, 21.1, 21.3, p.60.

[115] ibid, Ramainī, 23.2, p.63.

[116] ibid, Ramainī, 24.1-3, p.64.

[117] ibid, Ramainī, 25.1, p.66.

[118] ibid, Ramainī, 30.1, p.73.

[119] ibid, Ramainī, 31.1-3, p.76.

[120] ibid, Ramainī, 32.1-2, p.77.

[121] ibid, Ramainī, 33.3, p.78.

[122] ibid, Ramainī, 35.3, p.81.

[123] ibid, Ramainī, 50.3, p.104.

[124] ibid, Ramainī, 55.3-4, p.111.

[125] ibid, Ramainī, 62.1-3, p.120.

[126] ibid, Ramainī, 67.1-4, p.130.

[127] ibid, Ramainī, 69.3-5, p.134.

[128] ibid, Ramainī, 78.1-5, p.152.

[129] ibid, Śabda, 3.1-3, p.173.

[130] ibid, Śabda, 4.1-8, pp.174f.

[131] ibid, Śabda, 14.1-5, p.195.

[132] ibid, Śabda, 40.1-5, pp.244f.

[133] ibid, Śabda, 57.1-5, p.286.

[134] Bījaka, Ramainī, 1.1, p.1.

[135] ibid, Ramainī, 1.9, p.16.

[136] ibid, Ramainī, 1.11-12, p.17.

[137] ibid, Ramainī, 1.13, p.18.

[138] ibid, Ramainī, 2.1, p.20.

[139] ibid, Ramainī, 3.1, p.27.

[140] ibid, Ramainī, 3.4, p.29.

[141] ibid, Ramainī, 4.3, p.30.

[142] ibid, Ramainī, 4.4, p.30.

[143] ibid, Ramainī, 5.2, p.31.

[144] ibid, Ramainī, 5.4, p.32.

[145] ibid, Ramainī, 5.6, p.33.

[146] ibid, Ramainī, 6.1, p.33.

[147] ibid, Ramainī, 6.4, p.35.

[148] ibid, Ramainī, 7.2, p.36.

[149] ibid, Ramainī, 7.4, p.36.

[150] ibid, Ramainī, 8.1, p.37.

[151] ibid, Ramainī, 8.2, p.37.

[152] ibid, Ramainī, 9.2, p.39.

[153] ibid, Ramainī, 9.4-5, p.40.

[154] ibid, Ramainī, 20.2, p.58.

[155] ibid, Ramainī, 41.3, p.90.

[156] ibid, Ramainī, 51.1-3, p.105.

[157] ibid, Ramainī, 52.2-3, p.107.

[158] ibid, Ramainī, 58.1-4, p.115.

[159] ibid, Ramainī, 63.3, p.122.

[160] ibid, Ramainī, 66.1-2, p.129.

[161] ibid, Ramainī, 68.1-4, p.132.

[162] ibid, Ramainī, 70.1-3, p.135.

[163] ibid, Ramainī, 74.4, p.143.

[164] ibid, Ramainī, 75.1,6, p.147.

[165] ibid, Ramainī, 76.1-3, p.149.

[166] ibid, Ramainī, 77.1-3, pp.150f.

[167] ibid, Ramainī, 79.1, p.154.

[168] ibid, Ramainī, 80.1, p.155.

[169] ibid, Ramainī, 83.2, p.159.

[170] ibid, Śabda, 2.1-8, pp.167f.

[171] ibid, Śabda, 7.1-4, pp.180f.

[172] ibid, Śabda, 23.1-5, p.213.

[173] ibid, Śabda, 26.1-5, pp.220f.

[174] ibid, Śabda, 30.1-5, p.230.

[175] ibid, Śabda, 66.1-5, pp.304f.

[176] ibid, Śabda, 78.1-3, p.327.

[177] Bījaka, Śabda, 2, pp.167f;
also,
Kena Upaniṣad, 2-5.

[178] Bījaka, Ramainī, 74.5, p.143;
also,
Vivekacuḍāmaṇi, 59, p.21.

[179] Bījaka, Ramainī, 35.1, p.81; 70.1, p.135.

[180] ibid, Ramainī, 84, p.161;
also,
Bhagavadgītā, 2-62,63.

[181] Bījaka, Ramainī, 70.1, p.135; 30, pp.73f;
also,
Abhisamayālaṃkārāloka, p.61;
also,
Madhyamaka-śāstra, 18-9.

[182] Bījaka, Śabda, 12, p.191;
also,
Bhagavadgītā, 6-8.

[183] Bījaka, Ramainī, 20.3, p.58.

[184] ibid, Śabda, 16.5, p.200;
ibid, Ramainī, 32.1, p.77.

[185] ibid, Ramainī, 5.6, p.33;
also,
Kabīra Granthāvalī, p.4.

[186] Bījaka, Śabda, 40, pp.244f.

[187] Kabīra Granthāvalī, p.2.

[188] ibid, p.2.

[189] Bījaka, Śabda, 8, pp.182f.

[190] Kabīra Granthāvalī, p.81, p.104.

[191] Bījaka, Ramainī, 61, p.119.

[192] ibid, Śabda, 79.4, p.328.

[193] ibid, Śabda, 4, pp.174f.

[194] Kabīra Vacanāvalī, p.214 (as quoted in Kabīra Darśana, p.399);

also,

Kabīra Granthāvalī, p.209.

[195] ibid, p.127, p.196.

[196] Bījaka, Ramainī, 38.4, p.86;

also,

Kabīra Granthāvalī, p.58.

[197] Bījaka, Ramainī, 76, p.149.

[198] ibid, Śabda, 7.3, p.180;

also,

Kabīra Granthāvalī, p.109.

[199] Bījaka, Ramainī, 1,2, pp.1-26.

[200] ibid, Ramainī, 63.3, p.122;

Sākhī, 352, p.692.

[201] ibid, Śabda, 23, 213.

[202] ibid, Ramainī, 1, pp.1-18.

[203] ibid, Śabda, 27.4, p.222.
[204] ibid, Śabda, 11, p.189.
[205] ibid, Śabda, 41, p.246; 47, p.257; Ramainī, 62, p.120.
[206] ibid, Ramainī, 38.4, p.86.
[207] ibid, Ramainī, 61, p.119.
[208] ibid, Ramainī, 49.5, p.102.

Bibliography

1. *Abhisamayālaṃkārāloka,* Haribhadra, Gayakavar Oriental Series, Baroda.
2. *Ahamartha aur Paramārthasāra,* Swāmī Hariharānanda Sarasvatī (Karapātrījī), Svargāśrama Dhāma, Ara, 1962.
3. *Bhagavadgītā,* tr. Swami Gambhirananda, Advaita Ashrama, Pithoragarh, 1984.
4. *Bījak,* ed. Shrikrishnadas Khemraj, Venkateshvara Press, Bombay, 1904.
5. *Bījak,* ed. Shukdev Singh, Nilabh Prakashan, Allahabad, 1972.
6. *Brahma-Sūtra Bhāṣya of Śaṅkarācārya,* tr. Swami Gambhirananda, Advaita Ashrama, Pithoragarh, 1983.
7. *Kabīra-Darśana,* Dr. Ramjilal 'Sahayak', Lucknow University, 1962.
8. *Kabīra,* Hazariprasad Dvivedi, Rajkamal Prakashan, Delhi, 1973.
9. *Kabir and Kabir Panth,* G.H. Westcott, Baharatiya Publishing House, Delhi, 1974 (orig. pub. 1907).
10. *Kabīra Bhajanāvalī,* Pārakha Prakāśaka Kabīra Sansthāna, Allahabad.
11. *Kabīr Granthāvalī,* ed. P. N. Tivari, Hindi Parishad, Allahabad, 1961.
12. *Kabīra Kośa,* ed. Parashuram Chaturvedi and Dr. Mahendra, Smriti Prakashan, Allahabad, 1973.

13. *Kabīra Sāhitya kā Adhyayana,* Purushottamalal Srivastava, Sāhitya Ratnamālā Kāryālaya, Varanasi.

14. *Kabīra Sāheba kā Bījaka,* Hansdas Shastri and Mahabir Prasad, Kabīra Granth Prakashan Samiti, Barabanki, 1950.

15. *Kabīra Sāhitya kī Parakha,* Parashuram Chaturvedi, Bharati Bhandar, Allahabad, 1972.

16. *Kabīra-Vāṇī,* ed. Charlotte Vaudeville, Pondicherry, 1982.

17. *Kabīra Granthāvalī,* ed. Śyāmasundaradasa, Nāgarī Pracāriṇī Sabhā, Varanasi, 1954 (Saṁvat 2011).

18. *Kena Upaniṣad,* Gita Press, Gorakhpur.

19. *Madhyamaka-Śāstra,* Nāgārjuna, Mithila Vidyapeeth, Darbhanga, 1960.

20. *Sāhaityadarpaṇa,* Viśvanāthakavirāja, Motilal Banarasidass, Varanasi, 1956.

21. *Sant Kabīr,* ed. Ramkumar Varma, Sahitya Bhavan, Allahabad, 1966.

22. *Taittirīya Upaniṣad,* Gita Press, Gorakhpur.

23. *The Bījaka of Kabīra Sāheba,* with the commentary 'Bījakārtha - Prabodhinī', Śrī Prakāśamaṇināma Sāheba, Shri Kabīra Āshrama, Jamnagar, 1987.

24. *The Bījak of Kabīr,* tr. Linda Hess and Shukdev Singh, Motilal Banarasidass, 1986.

25. *The Nirgun School of Hindi Poetry,* P.D. Barthwal, The Indian Bookshop, Benaras, 1936.

26. *Vivekacūḍāmaṇi,* tr. Swāmī Madhavānanda, Advaita Ashrama, Pithoragarh, 1992.

27. *Yoga-Sūtra,* Bharti Vidya Prakashan, Varanasi, 1971.

www.ingramcontent.com/pod-product-compliance
Lightning Source LLC
LaVergne TN
LVHW061549070526
838199LV00077B/6971